Man without Memory

ILLINOIS SHORT FICTION

A list of books in the series appears at the end of this volume.

Richard Burgin

Man without Memory

UNIVERSITY OF ILLINOIS PRESS

Urbana and Chicago

FIC

Publication of this work was supported in part by grants from the Illinois Arts Council, a state agency.

The author wishes to thank Dean Thomas L. Canavan, Professor Dave Jones, Professor Burton Porter, Bill Henderson, Constance Decker Kennedy, and a special thanks to Linda K. Harris.

This book is printed on acid-free paper.

"Aerialist," first published in *Pequod,* December 1988

"Carlin's Trio," first published in *Southwest Review*, Autumn 1988

"Constitution Day," first published in *Shenandoah*, vol. 38, no. 3, December 1988

"Man without Memory," first published in a different form in *Confrontation,* no. 25–26, 1983

"Mason," first published in a substantially different form in *South Carolina Review,* vol. 16, no. 1, 1983

"New City," first published in *Confrontation,* no. 30–31, 1985

"Notes on Mrs. Slaughter," from *Pushcart Prize VII* and *Mississippi Review,* vol. 27, 1982–83

"The Opposite Girl," first published in *Confrontation,* no. 40, 1989

"The Victims," from *Pushcart Prize XI* and *Mississippi Review,* vol. 39, Spring 1985

R00703 96691

Library of Congress Cataloging-in-Publication Data

Burgin, Richard.
  Man without memory.

  (Illinois short fiction)
  I. Title. II. Series.
PS3552.U717M36   1989   813'.54   88–20864
ISBN 0–252–01602–5 (alk. paper)

*To my mother
and to the memory of my father*

Contents

Notes on Mrs. Slaughter

I'm living with Mrs. Slaughter in her apartment in Cambridge. She's not a bad housekeeper and now that the Mafia is beginning to leave her alone, she's regained her skill in cooking. Really I can't fault her at all. She doesn't even demand that I work, for example. Money is the farthest thing from her mind. For weeks I lived here without doing a thing, but then I began to feel guilty—I went out and got a job in the library stacking and sorting books. In the early stages of this situation I occasionally took walks (although Mrs. Slaughter hated to be left alone) even on the worst days of winter.

I don't want to rhapsodize unnecessarily about them but these were walks like no others I had ever taken. When you have no direction or specific conclusion in mind your walk is bound to be different. The colors, for instance, you take more note of them. You see that the snow isn't just white, or even predominantly white. You see all the black and gray there is in it, and you also see the blue. And the trees, even the birch trees have orange in them, as if part of them is always on fire. But nothing is so modified for me now as the sky. I would no longer say that the sky is blue, or the sky is gray. I see too many colors in it that there aren't even words for (for example, what color is the cross between salmon orange, tongue pink, and pebble pink), and so I have stopped talking about the sky.

Of course, if one sense is modified the others change also. For example, the sidewalk began to feel different. Sometimes I had the sensation that I was walking on a river, other times that it was rising over my my feet like quicksand. And the buses, the buses seemed to roar past me like tigers.

Once when I went to Harvard Square I began to read a newspaper in front of one of the outdoor magazine stands. Suddenly, I was overwhelmed by the work that went into producing it, the work that was in it. Afraid of bursting into tears, I quickly put it back on the stand.

Maybe there were too many newspapers in Harvard Square. That may be why I started to take the bus out to the suburbs, to Watertown and Newton and Waltham, and do my walking there.

I'll tell you what I saw there once. It was the warmest day of the winter and the snow was melting. A group of very old people, all of them over eighty, were out on their front lawn lining up for a picture. From across the street it was hard to tell how many of them were men, and how many were women. At a certain age the importance of that distinction begins to disappear. One of them, who held the camera, was arguing about how they should pose and soon a yelling match started. Insults were traded back and forth, and even when I inadvertently stopped and stared at them, it seemed to make no difference. No witness could deter them from their fight. Finally, they made a kind of compromise. They lined up in front of an oak tree, and smiling and holding hands, they held their pose so that the picture could be taken. Then all of them began to smile from ear to ear like choir boys. The sun was shining on their white heads, lighting them up like crystals. They began fussing over each other and soon they started taking pictures again, as if nothing could stop them, one after another—varying the pose just a little each time, the way models do on assignment.

. . . When I would go to the suburbs I'd naturally come back to the apartment later than when I'd walk around Cambridge. It was during those times that Mrs. Slaughter really suffered. She'd pace her floor, she'd fill up the bathtub with water only to empty it again, sounds would become amplified, even the air itself seemed to be full of Mafia fingers reaching for her throat.

She couldn't help cross-examining me. She wanted to know where I went on my walks, she wanted to know what I did. When my back was finally to the wall, when she fired one too many questions at me, I'd go to the mantel and take my pen, and an atmosphere of intense seriousness would suddenly descend.

It was a necessary defense, as well as being convenient. Of course, I couldn't have explained. Silence was the best course, I was sure of it.

So I continued my walks, I continued my rides, soon I began to go all over Massachusetts. Now how can I explain the things that happened? In Marblehead, for instance, as I was walking up and down those sloping roads that lead one away from the water, I stopped to look at a house that was white with dark green shutters and a little petunia garden in front. I looked at the wind blowing the petunias—what can I call those feelings?—I've had them before at zoos. I know that real astonishment is our deepest taboo—that even Spinoza would not consider wonder to be one of our emotions.

It was never difficult, after that day in Marblehead, to call up those feelings again. Sometimes it caught me unaware, in the most "incongruous" places. Once it happened in the urinal at the Boston Garden, another time waiting for the train to Park Street, when a man gave me a certain look as he was lighting a cigarette.

Little things, little acts could do it, you see, but still I kept up with my walking, even though it did take a lot out of me.

Now if I ever encountered a woman during my walks it was by pure chance. It would be something that happened to me, rather than something I caused, or even participated in. One of them I met during one of my rare walks through Boston. It was in the Boston Common, as a matter of fact. We met on the bridge, where the boats pass under in the spring and summer. I walked around the park with her for a few hours. She wanted to be something—a singer, a writer—I can't remember exactly what it was.

Probably because I said so little, she assumed that I liked her. She invited me to her apartment, and I followed along dutifully like her dog. I don't remember where she lived. I can't remember the exact location, but I do have a good picture of what her bedroom looked like. In fact, that turned out to be a problem. She was taking her clothes off, she'd gotten down to her bra and panties, and I was still fully dressed and staring at her bureau drawer at the little chips in the thin pink paint. Mistakenly thinking that I wanted her to undress me, she started undoing my belt, but I was already fascinated by the wood on her floor, by its delicate varnish and its slender cracks.

You see how it was. Finally she lay down on her bed with her legs apart. I watched her vagina for a few seconds, it looked like a miniature violin with a dull finish; to me the bed post proved much more fascinating, there was so much labor in it, so much time in it.

Things were made out of matter but things were also made out of time. Does that sound like a principle? I don't want to convey the impression that I have any. I wasn't trying to prove a thing with my walks, I'm almost positive of that. Supposedly philosophers have stopped asking what things are made of anyway. They want to know how things behave. Behavior is interesting—that's their slogan, apparently directing their lives.

. . . After a week or two of my walks I began to go to some restaurants, simply because as my walks got longer it became necessary to eat. Of course, I can't claim to be a connoisseur of good restaurants. I can't even say that I had a favorite place, but there was one cafeteria near Harvard where I went quite often, because no one noticed anyone else in there, and if I wanted to sit in solitude it was fine, and if I wanted to look at other people I could do that just as easily.

I never saw anything that made an indelible impression—oh, I saw lepers, queens, spastics, impassioned lesbians—but nothing that really left an imprint until I saw this fellow I'll call Mr. Egg. He was very tall, his neck was especially long, and he was thin. He looked as if he'd had a trauma, say in World War II. The remarkable thing about Mr. Egg, who sat in a corner near the water fountain and never dreamed he was attracting anyone's attention, was simply the way he ate his eggs. Or maybe I should say the way he didn't eat them, the way he guarded them. He stared at them reverently as if he were watching twin suns surrounded by a white cloud, then he would bend over them to almost eat them, but at the last moment he would refrain from touching them, the way a person may stop just short of touching a painting in a museum. How he loved those eggs! And what concentration. He was like a scientist laboring over chemicals, or a surgeon studying a heart. Nothing else existed but the eggs on his plate. No other reality was whole for him and he simply couldn't bear to disturb it, he would instead let the eggs grow cold as plastic while he never so much as touched them with his fork.

. . . I don't know why I wrote so much about Mr. Egg. Really, I only saw him there twice. Maybe I want to cling to my picture of him because it was, in a way, the last picture I had before I began to be chased.

I shouldn't say chased, because I was at first simply being followed. As I recall, I left the cafeteria one afternoon after watching Mr. Egg and I walked a few blocks toward the river, and then I realized that I was being followed—the same steps, the same shadow and sound.

I was surprised that I kept my equilibrium. I didn't even deviate from my course. I didn't, for example, bolt for a bus or else try to hail a taxi. Instead I kept my course straight for the river and my pursuer kept behind me, maybe a half a block behind, stopping to hide behind trees or else a parked car whenever it was necessary.

Quickly I searched myself. I was without any weapons. There was nothing in my pockets but a few small coins. Immediately I wondered why I was going toward the river. Wasn't this just what my pursuer would want? In fact I was sure it was the worst possible thing I could do.

I took a right at the stoplight instead of crossing the street. Nobody was walking on the bridge, but when I looked a second time I saw a little girl leaning over.

Would my change in direction be detected? Would it be discovered that I was walking in a circle? I reminded myself that it was important not to increase my speed. It was necessary to act as if I didn't know I was being followed.

It was very cold out. I hadn't dressed warmly enough—Mrs. Slaughter had offered me one of her sweaters but I walked out without taking it. The wind picked up. When it blew hard it seemed to go through my neck.

We were like soldiers in a procession, there was always the same distance between us. He is being polite, I thought to myself cynically. Quickly I envisioned a scenario for the pursuer's future actions. Probably it would be weeks, months, before I'd be taken. There would be phone calls first and no matter what ring I answered on the party at the other end would hang up. There would be perhaps some threats by mail, maybe even a rock through the window, though that seems too barbaric. Maybe this operation would go on only outdoors while I was walking. It would probably consist exclusively of trees and cars and steps and shadows, and nothing so abrasive as a phone would ever be employed.

So the chase by the river never came to pass. Instead I took the bus to Porter Square, as soon as I reached Harvard, and left my Pursuer behind. But all the way back to the apartment I wondered if he knew where I lived, if that information were already his property.

. . . Once in the apartment again, it wasn't long before I confessed everything that had happened to Mrs. Slaughter. This surprised me because I didn't think I would ever confide in her. Of course she had her own theory about it all. She was sure the Mafia had spotted me and had assigned a man to tail me. I didn't say anything to that. I never paid much attention to her anxieties about them, but in this case, while not accepting her explanation, I was willing to follow some basic rules to protect myself.

For one thing, we agreed to stay inside as long as our food held out. In light of this it was also necessary to keep the door and all windows locked, and to keep all the blinds down. Finally we decided to stay close to each other while we figured out what to do. The argument, such as it was, came down to this: either my Pursuer didn't know where we lived and had no way of finding out (in which case we were safe for now), or else he knew, in which case it would do little good to leave town. It was hard, of course, to determine just what he did know. Since we had to stay in the house there was little chance for any real scouting of our own. The only thing we could do was to peek periodically through a few inches of curtain at the street or at the alley in back, and these watches never produced a result.

The other thing Mrs. Slaughter asked of me was to stay in the same room with her all night, since I had developed the habit of pacing the floor at night and sometimes ended up sleeping on the living room couch. But as to what we did then, could one actually call it sleeping? We lay rigid and cold under the sheets with our eyes open like mummies.

Maybe one of us would get twenty minutes or so of sleep on occasion, but then the other one of us felt a special obligation to keep guard. Worst of all, perhaps, we hardly talked at all. Whether from fear of embarrassment I don't know, but we confined ourselves to abortive speculations about what we could do.

The apartment was like a dark aquarium now. In the daytime we moved by each other with our mouths closed like fish. If we opened our mouths it was to suck air rather than to talk. Even the feel of the skin on my body began to drop away from me, as I began to feel more like a fish.

Of course a fish still has a clock in its blood, it knows when to swim south, for example, but I had lost the clock too. Consequently, I did everything on impulse. I circulated around and around the house like a fish in an aquarium. Sometimes there would be an obstacle to go around but then I began to master the obstacles. In time I became familiar with every inch of my environment as I kept moving through it, varying only slightly the pattern of my passage each time, and also passing through with a perfect equilibrium— with exactly the same amount of tension, that remained as constant as the fixed temperature in a pool.

. . . At night, the darkness in the house doubled. We would take our food from the cabinets in the pantry because everything in the refrigerator, all the fruits and fresh vegetables, were rotten by then, and we had already run out of meats. We were eating out of cans exclusively. Unfortunately there was no milk or fruit juices. We had to eat dry cereal straight from the box, Cheerios and Sugar Pops without milk, and corn flakes. For our main meals we had tomato soup or ravioli, or canned pineapple, or tuna fish. We had no bread, only a half box of Triscuits.

After dinner we would light two candles and place them on the floor in the middle of the living room. Then we would lay down the game board of Chinese checkers or Parcheesi on a table and try to get through a game. Not only was it hard to finish our games because we had other things on our mind, but by evening we'd already played each of the games for about an hour in the daytime. There was nothing else to do, you see. Mrs. Slaughter didn't want to play any music. To us the record player was like a coral reef that cut into our space. It was a kind of intruder.

Once, after we finished our game, we began in a serious way, in quiet measured voices, to account for the time that had passed between my discovery of the Pursuer and our present discussion. How much calendar time, for example, had gone by? What had we done in those moments or what were we in those moments we were in? It was like investigating the history of a fish, like compiling the biographies of two fish in two different aquariums. In the aquarium there are no traces. A dog may leave tracks but fish never do. The water is always still, there is never a sign of motion.

No, we had to give it up, it was too much for us. We began instead to discuss our Pursuer. When we talked about him he became more astonishing, more real. One could not even say we had any emotions one way or the other toward him, though it would be wrong to say we regarded him as merely a force. But as soon as we got some insights into the Pursuer, we ceased talking about him, simply because we could not talk about him without referring to our safety, and the topic of safety was essentially beyond discussion. It was a double-headed monster—for to talk about safety was to talk about danger and we hardly needed to talk about that. It's true, we could make a run for it but we had no place to run to, no money to go anywhere with, and then we didn't want, really, to stick our heads out of the house. We were like termites now—we belonged in the house. If we could have we would have started living between the walls.

Besides, what assurance was there that the Pursuer wasn't waiting outside in the alley watching the house, wondering if we were in it or not, looking for a sign, a light, wondering what was going on behind the drapes, wondering if anything could be alive in such constant darkness? No, there was no assurance that that wasn't exactly what he wanted, that he wanted nothing more than for us to make a break for it. And he must have realized that we hadn't called in the police. Even if we had wanted to, there was nothing to show them—for the policeman was a man you had to show something to just like the fireman. He wasn't interested in your stories, he wanted evidence he could see with his eyes, he wanted proof. We had received no letters, no threats on paper or on the phone. To us the policeman was becoming even less substantial than a rainbow—he had the thickness of dew.

. . . I don't know how long the discussion lasted. At the end of it I suggested that we buy a gun. Mrs. Slaughter moved back a few steps from me when I said that so that I could hardly see her face.

. . . We didn't make any decision on the gun then. But don't think the gun left us. It floated over our heads while we circulated through the house. There were signs of it all over the aquarium. And when we ate, while we picked at our corn flakes or ravioli, the gun was beside it on our plates.

Then one afternoon while I was circulating, Mrs. Slaughter signaled to me with her index finger to come into her bedroom. Somewhat mystified and anxious, I obeyed her. When I was in front of her she suddenly opened her bureau drawer and showed me a pistol lying against a green felt cushion, like a strangely shaped jewel.

She felt compelled to explain why she'd concealed it from me, perhaps to keep my confidence in her strong. It hardly mattered that I told her I wasn't interested in her explanations. Nothing could stop her then. She took it as a trial. She said she'd had it for a long time, a good many months before I'd moved in. But it frightened her. She hated to show it to anyone, to admit to anyone that it was there in her room. Now that she'd exposed it, it would be different, she said, and as if to assure me, she cradled it in her arms.

The gun soon began to preoccupy her. She would keep it beside her plate as she ate breakfast in her underclothes. That, and the food on her plate, were the only realities for her now. She scarcely noticed that I existed. Of course, I could understand. For example, Mrs. Slaughter had gotten quite fond of ravioli, but that's how it is when you don't have much food and you stick to the same diet, you start to have love affairs with your food. They are strange affairs too, they are apt to be cruel, but in the end it is real love and there is no mistaking it or pretending otherwise. That's essentially what happened with Mrs. Slaughter and the ravioli. It began with aversion and from there to ambivalence, and there was even a long period where it seemed they were fighting. But underneath the constant bickering a passion was developing that was bound to surface sooner or later—that simply couldn't be denied.

The ravioli soon became like a theater to her. The actual eating was only part of it. She seemed fascinated by its form and color and would stare at it intensely for long intervals before placing even her fork on one of the pieces. Then she'd smell it, positioning her nose just a few inches above her plate, as if she were inhaling the most exquisite perfume. Also, she loved to touch it, and would feel several of the pieces from time to time. In a way I felt bad to merely eat my ravioli, and would have gladly given her some of my share, but I realized it would only detract from her theater. Part of her enjoyment, I realized, lay in watching me consume my portion. In fact, that was the only time, in those days, when she seemed aware of my existence.

But, you see, there wasn't enough food of any kind left to eat more than twice a day, and since we were still determined not to go out to get any more, the gun was, in a manner of speaking, far more important than food. The gun she could take with her while she took her hour-long bubble baths, and when she wanted to use the toilet she could hold it like a life saver in her hand.

And then at night while we were under the sheets listening for sounds of the Pursuer because she had said she'd heard him singing under our window one night, singing softly like a bird or a lunatic, at night the gun lay between us on the bed and she would periodically slip her hands over it and caress it until it seemed to lull her to sleep.

. . . While Mrs. Slaughter was so fascinated with the gun and the ravioli, I was becoming interested in the drapes. The drapes, I realized in a very intimate way, were protecting me and so I felt a sense of indebtedness to them. Also, at the same time, they were allowing me to investigate the situation, to peek through a few inches of the window and look at the snow on the streets, where I thought I might catch a glimpse of the pursuer.

I don't remember how many times I stared at the drapes, as if to discover the secret of their fiber. I do not know either how many times I parted them as if I were parting a woman's lips, just an inch or two to get a view of the outdoors. It is also difficult to know if the repetition of my actions increased my anxiety or diminished it.

The one thing I feel certain of concerning my relationship to the drapes is that there came a different stage when I realized rather deeply that while the drapes were in one sense protecting me (since they obstructed the Pursuer's line of vision into the apartment) at the same time they were calling attention to me, and maybe they were even tipping off the Pursuer.

Just as I began to mistrust the drapes, Mrs. Slaughter in time grew skeptical about the gun. First this showed simply in her reluctance to touch it anymore at night, when there was no light on. She was afraid it would go off; she was afraid it was loaded. It wasn't long before she refused to touch it at all, and so left it on the table without moving it, as if it were somehow sacred. When I suggested that she check to see if it were loaded, she grew petrified and then furious with me. Didn't I know that it might explode in her face while she was checking? Did I want her to go blind, or get scars like some of the other Mafia women? I didn't say anything to that. I was content to let it stay on the table where she'd look at it with an expression of both fear and longing.

. . . But soon she stopped watching it so much. We were beginning to play games again on the living room floor. At first we played backgammon but soon tired of it, and switched to Chinese checkers. Chinese checkers, you see, is not a game like backgammon where you can outwit your opponent and suddenly move ahead at the end of the game with a kind of O. Henry finish. There is no luck in Chinese checkers because you do not play with dice or cards. Each marble is an image of your mentality. It advances according to your design. The way we played, with each of us playing for three men, it took as long as a good game of chess.

But here there were also some drawbacks. After fifteen or twenty minutes there would be a big tie-up in the middle of the board. A series of blockades had caused it, and now it was difficult to move any of our pieces more than one space at a time. And sometimes we would have to move sideways or backward, sometimes at angles that didn't advance a piece but would merely permit a different piece in the near future the chance to advance two places. These are called preparatory moves.

. . . Several minutes later the blockades would multiply. We would be quiet and intense. We were laboring over our moves. Then I'd say, "Do you want to continue this tedium?"

She'd shake her head and we'd drink some vodka. Then we'd set the marbles spinning, set them free from their places, disrupting the board, and have a good laugh over it. We'd begin instead to play Parcheesi.

Parcheesi is a game played with dice and four pieces. A piece is always vulnerable and can be sent back to its starting point on any place on the board except the safety places. The object is to get all four men home. You can also form blockades in Parcheesi but they can never last for long because the pieces forming the blockade have to get home too. Parcheesi is a game of running and hiding and searching for safety. Above all it is a game of chance and chance lands on you like a thunderbolt. When you play while drinking vodka it is apt to make you laugh until you are hysterical. But when the hysteria wears off, you may have an empty feeling, you may even feel upset or frightened.

. . . And so we abandoned the games. For a while everything was quiet. Then we discovered, or rather we admitted what we had discovered for a long time, that there was no food left.

"This is the end of reality," I said to myself as I went outside in my overcoat. The walk consisted of two blocks to the nearest grocery store and then back. Except for one turn the walk would be a straight line.

. . . The light outside was brilliant yellow and white. The cold stung me and the light made me dizzy. My mission was to buy milk, cheese, eggs, bread, and, of course, ravioli. I walked briskly, like a man who wants to catch a train but is too dignified to run. I hardly allowed myself to think about what I was doing. It was only later, maybe two hours after we ate, that I dared to think about what had happened. Mrs. Slaughter was taking another bath and I was alone on the couch. But it wasn't fear I felt then. Suddenly I had a picture of myself walking through the snow with the bag of groceries. It was so beautiful, why hadn't I looked around and seen more of the outdoors?

True, I did get some reward for my daring venture. Mrs. Slaughter lavished a lot of attention on me. She became suddenly very affectionate and kept kissing me on the neck.

Is it any wonder, then, that the next morning I went out on another walk?

This time I saw green and white houses on the snow. I saw a car sputtering out of its driveway like an angry little whale. I saw sand spread out on the sidewalks like caviar and little girls walking to school with their green school bags over their shoulder, and the gray oatmeal-colored sky where two dark clouds hung like ships about to converge, over them and over all.

I saw a butcher's shop, a dry-cleaning store, a liquor store with its orange neon sign. I saw a shopping center with stores as wide as mountains. I saw the procession of people that passed in and out of the stores like fish in the sea. I examined them closely, as if I expected them to be a hallucination. The woman in the black kerchief who had just bought some lamb chops and was heading toward her car as if it might be on fire, I strained to see the color of the mole above her chin, as if it might lend her some more dignity.

It was stunning, humbling, beautiful, and humiliating to walk around. I looked at the Star Market—suddenly so sturdy, so much time in it, a somber and compact paradise. I looked at the sky and back at the ground in front of my feet and then back at the sky again. I felt hopeless, dizzy, in the moment I was in the Pursuer was gone! . . . I continued to look, first at the telephone wires as thin as necklaces and I tried to imagine how the signals traveled through them. Then I watched the people on the far corner, so unafraid of each other, so trusting as they waited for their bus.

. . . I began to walk up the sidewalk looking into all the store windows as I passed the liquor store, the drugstore, and the camera shop. I turned the corner. In the last window a man was throwing a pizza in the air. I looked at my feet, my black shoes as they walked over the snow.

. . . In the next moment I began to succumb to a strange feeling of helplessness. It was hard to know who I was. Nothing can threaten identity like a flight into ecstasy—no matter how brief. It was almost with relief, then, though I was still afraid, that I saw him trailing after me again driving a long black car. I turned a corner heading back to Mrs. Slaughter's and the Pursuer followed me. I couldn't resist turning around to try and catch a glimpse of him, but the driver was wearing dark glasses, and besides he was too far away.

Constitution Day

1

When my brother was about eight and I was thirteen, he began covering himself up. He kept a shirt on all the time, even through the summer, and wore rubber slippers over his feet on the beach. When he had to take a bath he'd wear a long white cotton bathrobe both into and out of the bathroom. If I ever saw an inch of his underpants he'd get visibly nervous, or angry, although he'd never say a word about it.

My mother, who worries about everything, started worrying about this. She was going to send him to a child psychologist, which was even more in vogue then than it is now, but my father interceded. He said he'd find out what the problem was his own way. One day when we were driving back from the Cape, he asked Darren if he'd mind taking his shirt off in front of our dog, Cuddles. I laughed, but Darren looked hurt and became eerily quiet. Finally he said, "I think your joke was pointless and insensitive."

My brother was verbally precocious and could rip off an impressive sentence like that every now and then. Five minutes later my father stopped at a Howard Johnson's and gave me some money to buy an ice cream. That's when Darren told my parents that he only covered up because of me, and to prove it he defiantly took off his shirt, which he put back on as soon as I returned to the car.

2

Darren and I went to the same grammar school and high school in Brookline. I was a straight A student and Darren got mostly B's and

C's, yet he was, at times, almost treated like a prodigy. His mediocre success in school was actually used as further confirmation of his extraordinary intelligence. In other words, because he could rattle off these funny and sometimes dazzling one-liners, people assumed he was smarter than his classmates and that school just wasn't challenging enough for him.

Darren had one other ace in the hole: he was a master at games and was virtually unbeatable at Scrabble, gin rummy, and later at chess. Often I'd end up doing his homework as a result of losing yet another of those endless contests. I didn't really mind that, because Darren was always very grateful. As little brothers go he wasn't mean, but he was secretive (bordering on sneaky) and oh so vain. Typically, when he finally did take his shirt off and begin swimming (he was about twelve then) he discovered that in short distances he was faster than me. Immediately he began challenging me to races at the Cape, which of course he'd win repeatedly.

I don't want to leave the impression that all our times at the beach were so dismal—that would be a great untruth. For instance, I remember one day when my family took a trip to Provincetown. My parents were very involved with each other, and Darren and I took a walk away from them to the sand dunes. One of us would climb to the top of a dune and jump off, rolling close to the foot of the other, who was watching. I think it was the first summer Darren took his shirt off. We took turns jumping and watching and finally we were having such a good time we began jumping off together. Probably it was one of the happiest times of my life. In fact, by concentrating on it I'm sometimes able to use it to help me sleep on those nights when I have insomnia.

3

I wasn't surprised that Darren lost his virginity when he was only fifteen. I always assumed he'd do well with women. He had dark good looks and was attractively skinny. Also, there's something in the female heart (at least there was in those days) that's drawn to a person like Darren who seems brilliant but a little reckless. It's that missionary impulse. (I know a number of men, for that matter, associates in my firm, who still can't resist certain women they think they can save or reform.) I'm sure that's why my mother, despite her best intentions, couldn't help spoiling Darren. She saw all this exciting potential and must have thought if she tried a little harder she could bring it out. When you think about it, perpetually untapped potential can be a great weapon.

I also wasn't surprised that after his first affair there were lots of other women. Not that my brother was ever flip or methodical about them. He suffered a lot for women and would even love them for a short time in his own way. Since he didn't have a good rapport with my father, who was career-obsessed in any event, and since my mother was extremely puritanical, I was the recipient of Darren's girl stories. He'd tell me all the details, even the compliments women gave him in bed, which were rather hard for me to hear when I was still a virgin.

With no such stories of my own to tell (I was far too proud to invent any), I confided my career goals instead—the fellowships I was applying for, the contacts in law school I was pursuing, and later, my cases at the firm. It's also true that after my wife's miscarriages Darren was wonderful to me and let me pour my heart out about my marriage with Beth. I remember being surprised and touched that he would listen as well as he did. There's nothing so touching as seeing an injustice rectified, and at the time I felt that kind of listening corrected a serious imbalance between us. Later I realized that it was my fault for not talking about Beth earlier, that Darren always would have listened and may never have known when he was hurting me, that I've often expected a stab in the back from him when he's never even picked up the dagger.

4

Although he ended up working as a free-lance contractor, a job in which he has no meaningful contact with language, years ago Darren used to be quite adept at telling stories. He hardly ever finished any—it was typical of my brother to invent premises and then abandon them—but he had an undeniably strong imagination. Once when he was about sixteen, he called me into his room to tell me his latest idea for a story, perhaps even a novel he intended to write.

"Here's the plot," he said excitedly as he paced around his room. "A man grows up convinced that everything that happens in the world is solely for his education and benefit. He believes that God is staging this 'show,' in other words, for him alone. Later he thinks that a few other people have the same fate and that he'll know them when he sees them. Anyway, some of the consequences of his belief system are that he's totally ambivalent about his career because the people who judge his work really only exist to influence his development. It's the same with women. He's afraid of love since the women he meets are also only characters in a play performed for him, with no real destiny of their own."

I don't remember what I said to him about his story. I'm sure I was both angry and astonished since I immediately realized he was describing himself and what he thought of as his own tragic fate.

. . . I'm thinking about all this on a half-full train to Philadelphia, with absolutely no one to talk to. In fifteen minutes Darren will be meeting me at the station. It's Constitution Day—a very big deal in Philadelphia—and he's invited me to stay with him for a day or two while my wife's visiting her parents. Though I meet him in Philadelphia at least once a month, I haven't stayed overnight in quite a while and I'm excited about it. In time I even (perhaps inevitably) start imagining what Darren would think if the situation were reversed and he were on a train thinking about me. This game ends abruptly, however, with the announcement that we'll be in the 30th Street Station in three minutes. For the first time there is some rustling about on what seemed a train full of corpses.

5

I'd hardly put my things in his apartment when Darren insisted we watch the Constitution Day parade, even though there was a steady rain outside.

"Just grab an umbrella, David," he said, pointing to his closet. As usual, his closet is a barely contained chaos.

"If you're going to send me on a safari at least provide me with a guide," I said, and Darren laughed the high-pitched slightly hysterical laugh that he's had his whole life and only uses when he's truly delighted. I have to admit this laugh always melts me, seems to melt away years of anxiety, so that I feel temporarily like I'm sixteen and on the way to Fenway Park or to the movies with Darren—and indeed, I'm now going to a parade with him.

We walk briskly in the light rain down Chestnut Street toward Penn's Landing, where the ceremony is going on. It's odd to feel so buoyant and happy but I tell myself to just enjoy it, that there are so few times like this that there's no point in analyzing it. On the other hand, that's just what makes it frightening—these moments are so scarce that I sometimes panic when they happen. Also, I'm forced to realize that they only happen when I see my brother. Maybe they happened during my first years with Beth, though there was so much anxiety as well that it wasn't exactly the same thing, but now they only happen when I see Darren. Of course, it's absurd to brood like this just because I've been suddenly attacked by a little happiness, but I find I have to think about *something* to mute it a bit, so I resume the game I was playing in the train where I tried to guess Darren's thoughts about me. I decide that Darren would probably admit to being jealous of my marriage and of my relative financial success. (I'm a divorce lawyer and a junior partner in the firm.) Maybe he'd also think that as a child I was favored by our father. He's hinted at that to me before. Undoubtedly, he would still express deep sorrow for my wife's miscarriages and possibly also regret making fun of my wearing glasses and being overweight when we were kids.

"Just a block to go," Darren says, with a touch of anxiety in his voice, and I immediately stop my game. Neither of us sees any signs of a crowd, and when we get to 6th Street we learn that the ceremony, as well as the president's address at Independence Mall, has been sectioned off for ticket holders. So we stay under the awning of a laundromat and watch a stoic band from Ohio State get steadily rained on. Every now and then the band yells out some signals or code words to demonstrate their discipline but it isn't very entertaining. Behind them is an all-black band from New Orleans. At ten-minute intervals the players drop their instruments and do a thirty-second dance and the crowd politely applauds, while a tiny sprinkling of confetti falls from a few windows.

. . . "Excuse me, sir," Darren says to a tall black man in a ripped raincoat. "Do you know where the rest of the parade is?"

The black man has silver-flecked hair and a long cigarette dangling from his lips. My brother fingers his mustache while he waits for an answer. "City Hall," he says, pointing west. Darren thanks him then turns to me saying, "You heard the man." Darren is wearing a beige trench coat and still looks athletically trim. While we walk I notice the same long, youthful stride he's had since he was a teenager.

At City Hall they've set up grandstands which are pretty full. Two Rolls Royces pass by. In one is Chief Navajo, an Indian dignitary I'd never heard of; in the other is Walter Cronkite. They're followed by a giant float that has the flags and seals of the first thirteen states. A number of actors in Revolutionary War costumes are on board. This float, which is kind of clever, is sponsored by Merrill Lynch.

Of course, Darren dumps on the parade mercilessly. Although he actually loves parades, he somehow feels compelled to make fun of them. (He used to do the same thing when we'd go to the Boston marathon as kids.) After a few more floats, however, we have both had enough of the parade and decide to have a drink. We walk into a bar on 16th Street. As soon as we get settled in a corner he asks me his obligatory questions: How am I? How is Beth? How's my work?

When I was about sixteen and still sure that Darren had no interest in listening to me I grabbed him by the shirt one day and said, "If you ever want to talk to me again you're going to ask *me* some questions about myself first. It can't always be just about you." It was one of the few times I ever touched my brother, and his face drained of color. A moment later he walked out of the room. Of course I said I was sorry, but from then on he's ritualistically asked me about my health, etc., at first out of fear, then later sarcastically, when it became a joke between us. Even now he always unselfconsciously and quite sweetly asks me these obligatory questions. Sometimes it annoys or embarrasses me and I think about protesting and putting an end to what I began twenty years ago. This time, however, I find it oddly touching and I answer that my health is good. "I've been playing a lot more tennis at the club," I add, "though I'll never be any competition for you."

Darren looks genuinely embarrassed and says, "You've always

had an exaggerated opinion of me, probably because of all my exaggerations.''

We laugh and I begin to answer him about my job. I'm about halfway through describing my latest case with a vice president of a new video distributing corporation when a woman at the next table, who I hadn't noticed before, asks Darren for a light.

''Sure,'' he says, producing a lighter from his pocket and lighting her cigarette.

''I hope it's okay if I smoke?''

''Of course it's okay. Did you come from the parade?'' he asks, and just like that they start talking.

I give the woman a fairly penetrating stare but she avoids my eyes. She looks mid-thirtyish to me and has honey blonde hair (probably natural) and hazel eyes, which are almond-shaped and are easily her best feature. Her eyes are set off with a good deal of eyeliner, however, and she's wearing light purple lipstick—nothing outrageous, mind you, but not exactly demure either.

While she and Darren exchange jokes about the lackluster parade she manages to slip off her raincoat. She's wearing a yellow summer dress (no straps) and has a small bust, but apparently isn't inhibited from wearing something that shows off half of it. All this is upsetting me, although I shouldn't be upset or surprised since this type of thing happens to Darren a lot.

After they finish making fun of the parade and discussing its possible impact on the mayoral race, they introduce themselves and then Darren finally introduces me. The woman's name is Claire. She smiles more brightly than she needs to when we shake hands. I immediately drop my eyes and recede into my chair while she and my brother start discussing their apartments and then Philadelphia real estate in general. (I am wondering if he will describe himself as an architect or, more accurately, as a contractor when the time comes.)

However, my mind wanders and I don't find out if the time comes or not. When I refocus on the situation I look at my watch and let three more minutes pass before I excuse myself to go to the men's room. Claire smiles at me as I get up from the table and Darren has a slightly worried expression in his eyes.

In the men's room I stand in front of the urinal trying to talk myself out of my state of mind. There is no reason to feel angry. All he's doing is talking. If the situation were reversed, if I didn't have Beth, I'd have to depend in part on these kinds of meetings myself. I have to remember that, because I'm used to Beth, I take her a little for granted, and of course I'm no longer as excited by her as I once was. But I made a choice. I wanted someone I could trust and depend on. I would be terrified to live my brother's kind of life, especially now with all the diseases around. And even if there weren't any I'd be afraid of being alone. I always was.

Certainly it's not that I don't have sympathy for his kind of love life, despite my own record of relentless fidelity. Quite the contrary. I'm thinking, for example, as I sometimes do, of Margo F., whom I represented eight years ago in a suit against her much older husband, a prominent investment banker whose aspirations for young models were almost as strong as his appetite for money. It was just before I was coming up for a partnership in the firm, and the case was one of those rare examples of perfect timing in my life for we expected a lot of money from the settlement. Margo was tall and blonde, twenty-six, fiendishly attractive, and extremely self-possessed. She exuded the kind of confidence that wilts some men but thrills others. She was also a masterful flatterer. In our first meeting she referred to me twice as a "hugely successful attorney" and mentioned "the sensational job" I'd done representing a show business acquaintance of hers.

Of course I didn't let myself have any personal feelings for her. I doubt that I even allowed myself to look closely at her during our initial conversations, not even when she broke down crying while discussing her husband's infidelities. On the other hand, I didn't tell Beth about her, nor Darren, although in many ways he is still my chief confidant. When Margo canceled our fourth appointment five minutes before I expected her and then suggested I come to her penthouse on Sutton Place on some silly pretext, I didn't argue. Not with several million dollars involved. I merely considered it one of the irresponsible indulgences that comes with the territory, as they say.

There was a martini waiting for me when I arrived. It seemed we were completely alone.

"Sorry to put you through so much trouble, David."

"Don't mention it," I said.

"You're just as kind as I'd heard you were."

I thanked her again. She was wearing a magnificent apricot colored business suit, which I appreciated while struggling against a vindictive erection. We talked about nothing in particular for a few minutes. I admired her view of the East River and she suggested I walk over to the wall-length windows at the far end of the living room to see it better while she "changed into something less formal." On the way I noticed two small original paintings by Jasper Johns.

A few minutes later I heard Margo return, heralded by her high heels, but I didn't turn around until she said, "How do you like the view?" She was wearing a Japanese print silk blouse, and nothing else, except a pair of quasi-transparent pink panties, and her shoes. Her blouse was open and ended at her waist. I noticed that her legs were longer and even more curvaceous than I'd imagined and her breasts fuller too. Why was this happening? I was speechless but she was quite composed, as if we were both members of a nudist colony. She picked up her drink from the table, without breaking stride, as she walked toward me. I think her composure, her colossal, utter self-confidence shocked me as much as her nudity. She offered me her drink but I declined. Then she reached up delicately and ran her fingers through my hair (I remember regretting that I wore glasses) before I stepped back, almost against the window. I spoke more rapidly than I would in a courtroom but just as distinctly.

"Mrs. F., let me say two things. I consider you the most beautiful woman I have ever seen but I'm a very happily married man."

She looked at me for a second and smiled ironically. "Fine. I thought we had something, but fine, I must have misread you. I'll see you in your office tomorrow at three o'clock sharp," she said, inventing her appointment on the spot.

"I'll be there," I said, as I tried to remember who I'd now have to cancel in that time slot. She turned and walked with the same walk-in-the-park speed she'd maintained when she approached me. I kept my back to her as I heard the clip clop of her heels across the long marble floor. Finally I turned for a split second and got an enduring view of her perfect rear end. A moment later she turned around herself, "I expect you to get me this home and everything in it, no less than three million dollars outright, and a half-million dollars a year for the next seven years."

"I can do that."

"Fine. Can you see yourself out now?" She left the living room, which seemed as long as a football field, and as I started toward the door I thought of Darren, that he had had women as beautiful as Margo, that he never would have refused her no matter what, whereas I was completely imprisoned by my values, that indeed she should have met him and perhaps even would if I were foolish enough to arrange it. I could not even experience myself alone in that moment, so supremely untypical of my life. Instead I took refuge in my little brother, the impossible-to-get-rid-of Darren!

Then, of course, it was back to the office, where the secretaries and paralegals were, as usual, impeccably deferential toward me. One of them said my wife had called (this was shortly after her last miscarriage when she was calling the office a lot). But I didn't call back right away. Instead, shaking and humiliated, I went straight to the bathroom (the origin of all our humiliations when you think about it). I looked at myself in the mirror. Was I going to cry or laugh hysterically? I was going instead to masturbate, a quick, no-nonsense, soundless orgasm in one of the stalls, while I closed my eyes and saw again Margo's walk across her endless marble football field.

. . .The faucet has been running, I've taken off my glasses and quite unconsciously cleaned them about sixteen times and then washed my face a few times for good measure. Why does seeing Darren cause me to have all these steamy memories? It's ridiculous in a way. Meanwhile he'll think I'm having some kind of awful attack in the bathroom.

Just before I finally do leave the men's room I wonder if he'll still be there, if he won't instead have run off with his little pickup, leaving a note with a drawing on it, perhaps on a napkin, to explain it all. But when I return he's sitting alone.

"Where's your eclair?" I say as I sit down. There is a new drink in front of me.

"Oh. She had to go."

"I thought you might have gone with her."

"Are you kidding? David, be serious."

I notice that my left hand is shaking, so I keep it under the table.

"You never told me how Beth is," Darren says.

"Beth is fine."

"You two love birds happy as ever?"

"I don't know that we're exactly birds, Darren."

"What's the matter, David?"

At first I shrug, but he asks me again.

"That woman you were talking to upset me."

"Why?"

"I don't know. I thought you might leave with her. I thought she was some kind of prostitute."

"David, listen to me. A. I would never do that to you. B. I'm not interested in prostitutes—not in 1987. C. You're inadvertently insulting me, because A. I would never do that to you."

"Sorry. I don't know why I'm being so jumpy."

"Come on, let's shake," Darren says in his earnest voice, as if shaking hands is the most wonderful thing there is to do on earth. He extends his hand over the top of the table and I meet it with my right hand, which isn't shaking. . . .

The handshake itself is quite solemn but Darren immediately begins joking and laughs so hard once that he spills some of his drink. Despite his attempt at light-heartedness, it is awkward after the handshake. We try to change the subject, we even eventually succeed in changing the subject, but we are both feeling guilty and apologetic and tense until I just want to stop talking about it and get out of the bar. Luckily Darren feels the same, and a minute later he suggests going home.

Outside the rain has stopped and a few stars are out. The wind is moving the clouds and the trees by the playground we pass. We start talking about the pennant race, united by our mutual loathing of the Mets. My brother looks very handsome with the wind tossing his hair around. Although I see Darren about twice a month, I can never quite get used to how handsome he is.

Darren lives in a small studio in a high-rise which he says he can afford less every year. When we get back he makes us some scrambled eggs and toast and decaffeinated coffee. While he's in the kitchen, which is so small it can barely contain the two of us, I ask him about his work. He tells me that it's spiritually deadening and that financially it's the worst it's been in three years. My brother is one of those few people who are genuinely more gifted than what they've trained for or can actually get. This is, naturally, unspeakably frustrating for him, so I decide to swallow what I was going to say about it being my best earning year yet.

After we eat we talk about going to the movies but decide to stay in and watch TV. A lot of times things are so tense at the office that when I get home all I want to do is watch TV, yet I can't remember the names of the specific shows. It's the same with Beth, who's under a great deal of pressure at the company she works for. She doesn't know the names of the shows either. But Darren does know the names and gives me a little summary of the available fare. We end up watching the end of a movie on HBO and then the eleven o'clock news, which leads off with a story on the Constitution Day parade. Just as they're showing the floats the telephone rings and Darren hops up from the bean bag he's sitting on and takes it on the second ring. I can hear him laughing and talking in his warm telephone voice. A couple of minutes later he walks, phone in hand, into the kitchen.

I'm certain the call is from a woman—Darren does not have, to my knowledge, any male friends—but it's futile to speculate on who she might be, for he rarely identifies his girlfriends these days. Still, something tells me that it is Claire. He probably said something to make her excited back in the bar and now she's calling to see if I'm still here or still awake or to see if they might get together later. And maybe now that he has fed me, made up his bed for me (he's insisted on sleeping on a cot), Darren will slip out on some pretext and see her.

When he gets off the phone the sports segment of the news is over and the weather is half through.

"Who's the late caller?" I say from the reclining chair, the one piece of nice furniture in an apartment crammed with old movie posters (James Dean, Elvis, Humphrey Bogart), sports paraphernalia, old movie magazines, and manuscript pages that may or may not be his stories.

"Was it Claire?" I say before he can answer.

Darren blushes slightly. "No, it's a lady friend named Lucy."

"Lucy!" I say, pulling the reclining chair upright and turning to look at my brother who is standing under a Marx Brothers' poster in the kitchen. For some reason I repeat her name two more times.

"And do you love Lucy?"

"No, not that way," he says, smiling his sheepish smile. "She's just a good friend and kind of a contact. She called from California."

"California?"

"Los Angeles." He walks out of the kitchen now and sits at the table where we ate the eggs. "It was something I wanted to talk to you about. She works in an agency, actually she's a part owner, and she's offered me a position there."

"She's offered you a position? Sounds sexy. Doing what?"

"Reading scripts mostly. Evaluating them as potential clients or properties. Anyway, I think I'm going to do it."

I ask him how they met and he says he met her in Philadelphia and that she moved to L.A. five years ago. He's vague about the details, so I assume they were lovers. Darren never has completely platonic friendships with women. I have gotten out of the chair by now and find myself pacing off a little rectangle as I ask my brother a rapid series of questions about this job, the last one being how definite the offer really is.

"It's definite. I'll have to take a cut in pay, and it's more expensive out there, but why should I stay here? I'm going nowhere in my work, I can't even call it a career. I'm very unhappy here, David, truly unhappy. Why shouldn't I try to make myself someone, the way you have? I'd like a nice home and a wife too, but that costs money, doesn't it?"

"But what exactly do you know about agenting?"

"I'll just have to be able to evaluate scripts at first, which I know I can do."

"And live with her?"

He has that crestfallen expression again. "That's uncalled for. I told you, we're just friends."

"Sorry."

"Look, it's a new profession, no getting around that. But I feel confident I can learn it. Maybe I'll even have a chance to sell my own screenplays. Who knows.''

I look at him closely for a moment and realize that, of course, that's the real reason.

''Well this has been a night of surprises.''

''I hope they haven't all been bad ones.''

''California is a bit of a surprise.''

''I did plan to tell you about it. It's one of the reasons I wanted to see you. Believe me, I went over the pros and cons hundreds of times. It's probably the most carefully thought-out decision of my life.''

''Then you've definitely decided to go?''

Darren turns to look at me and I'm struck again by the beauty of his face. He looks like neither of my parents really, who have ordinary faces like mine.

''Yes, David, I have.''

I ask him when he plans to leave and he says in a month when his lease is up. Then I ask him if he's told our parents yet and I think he says he sent them a letter yesterday. The reason I can't tell for sure is that I'm preoccupied with my own train of thought and have turned around facing the windows. I'm thinking that there is still time. I have a month to work on him and I will scare him silly about California. Of course I also realize it would be counterproductive to start now, so instead I tell my brother I wish him well and will help him if he needs it, in any way I can. Then I suggest we keep watching TV, which seems to greatly relieve him.

We turn on ''Johnny Carson'' but my mind is still in a whirl. For one thing, Darren's equanimity—the way he's laughing so easily at Carson's monologue, completely absorbed, the California question apparently totally resolved for him—is making me angry. How is it that at this stage of his life he's decided to throw away everything to follow some childish fantasy in Hollywood and all because of some woman he managed to completely conceal from me? And why does it fall upon me to suffer about it and set things right—for I can't imagine either of my parents doing a thing about it?

When the pressure of these thoughts gets too intense I try another line of argument to calm myself down. I think, It's not as if he were going to Europe. I can still visit him, though I'll have to adjust to seeing him much less often and he'll still seem profoundly missing. But this line is off the point, which remains that Darren, who's been relatively under control, is about to suddenly destroy his life.

. . . At the end of "Johnny Carson" my brother goes to sleep on the cot next to the bed. I told him I wanted to read for a while, but despite the effort I made to calm down, I still can't concentrate and for several minutes all I do is watch him sleep. He's pulled the blankets so high he's almost completely covered up. It's the same way he's slept since he was a child.

. . . Finally I walk over to the window and look at the night lights. Then I reach into my sports jacket and remove my pocket mirror, and as I suspected my face is flushed. When my face is flushed I look older, I get jowls and truly look my age. I put the mirror away and shut off the kitchen light I was supposed to be reading by. Then I get this crazy thought: In a world of two people it wouldn't matter what you look like, it wouldn't matter, for instance, that Darren is handsome and I'm not. Categories like that can only exist with three people. It's the third one who always judges the other two.

. . . Now I'm really thinking like a first-class idiot, I say to myself. It must be time to go to sleep. But once I take off my glasses my eyes stay open and I start thinking about Beth. Of course there'll be no way to hide the news about Darren when I see her. She'll know without asking me, the way she knew how I felt after her miscarriages. There's no possibility of hiding anything from her—the only thing I ever hid was that afternoon with Margo F. and that was only because I *knew* I'd never do anything with Margo anyway. It's funny how over time sex diminishes, how excitement and fun and companionship itself diminish but the knowledge of each other beats on like a regular heartbeat until you discover that's what you're ultimately married to. So from this knowledge she'll say, "Maybe it will be a good thing for Darren to move. Anyway, what can you do?" Which is her way of saying you only want your brother to stay in Philadelphia for yourself, and I will have to acknowledge that she has caught me being selfish again and that I'll have to do the unselfish thing and let him go.

Thinking about all this I feel chilled, like a north wind has suddenly entered my veins, and I reach down in the dark and grab the sheet and blankets and pull them above my waist, then over my shoulders until they're up to my ears. I roll over on my back and listen to Darren sleeping in the dark. He's breathing so delicately it's as if he's afraid of disturbing someone else. It's extraordinary how quiet he is. There could be a fly next to him, the most jittery creature on earth, and it wouldn't be disturbed. Instead, it would sleep right next to him the whole night.

New City

The rain's over. I heard it end an hour ago but I didn't expect a sky like this. It reminds me of California. Day after day there'd be cloudless blue skies like Xeroxes of each other. But those skies were never deep blue like today's sky, or like so many skies are in the East. I'm living in Philadelphia now. It's my fourth city in six years. I keep getting these one-year teaching jobs and of course I have to go where the work is. When I moved in a week ago it was gray and humid. The weather stayed that way all week in a kind of holding pattern until it finally rained. Meanwhile I spent the whole week organizing my stuff. I arranged my books and records alphabetically by author and composer. Actually, I arranged everything in my apartment alphabetically. I wanted everything to be organized, although I've never cared that much before, not even when I was in New York where people often treat their apartment like it's their art form.

There's not much time before classes begin and I'd planned to do some work, but once I saw the sky everything changed. My windows are too small or else their position on the walls is too low for me to see the whole sky, but I could infer it. Well, I'll have to go outside now, I said to myself. Cloudless blue skies have the effect of making me feel very sorry for myself if I'm not outside. Also, if I stay inside the thought of the sky overstimulates my memory, and I end up thinking of things I'm better off forgetting.

There's a park across the street from me. I saw it from the front seat of the van when I drove up here with the movers from New York. The next day when I went shopping I looked a little more closely and saw some kids playing basketball. I remember thinking I might want to play after I finish shopping but my shopping put me in a bad mood. It was a regular market called Unimart, but it was crowded with returning college students. I hated looking for so many things, then gathering them up one by one, then having little conversations with myself about what to buy or what not to buy and what brand name and so forth. I also didn't like standing in line with everyone around me young enough to be my kid. So I was in no mood for basketball when I got out.

That was really the last time I went outside until today. But the basketball players stuck in my mind. So now I'm putting on a pair of sneakers and some shorts under my pants and I take a towel and a few other things like a book to read, in case I can't get in a game.

It's a big park. It's not Central Park, but in the context of the neighborhood it looks big. On my way to the courts I pass several people sitting alone, one to a bench, not doing much of anything. Then when I'm about a hundred yards away I see seven basketball players. They're all black and they're all at least ten years younger than me. I'm in my early thirties, just young enough by a year or two for it not to be embarrassing to care so much about playing basketball. In basketball I can get embarrassingly competitive.

For about five minutes I watch them shooting, to sort of feel out the situation. I move up closer until I'm about forty feet away but still on the grassy part of the playground. I'm thinking that we could play four-on-four, but they don't look over at me once.

Then I notice a little black kid about twelve shooting alone at the opposite basket. I take my pants off and carry my things to a safe spot near the basket and walk out on the court and start shooting with him. He's wearing green pants and a Ghostbusters T-shirt and he's about five-foot four. Every time he misses a shot he blames it on the angle of the sun or the lopsided rim or the wooden backboards. I don't say much to him although I think he's a cute kid. Whenever I sink a jumper I look over at the older players to see if they've noticed but I only catch one of them half looking.

Then two more black guys around eighteen come on the court. One of them shoots with me and the little kid; the other joins the seven players at the opposite basket. Next thing I know someone says "Let's go full" and everyone, including me, starts shooting at the foul line where the older players had been shooting. A band of about five little black kids suddenly emerges to get in line too. The idea is: the first two to make the shot become captains and pick four other players for their team. The situation always produces a lot of self-conscious joking, especially when players miss, as six of the first seven do.

When it's my turn to shoot someone says: "The white dude's gonna make it, watch this, he's gonna make it."

Of course I ignore the comment. Even in games that are all-white I always assume an attitude of mature indifference. So I slip into my attitude, but I'm feeling a little tension too. I don't really expect to make the shot and I don't, although I don't miss badly. My shot hits the back rim and bounces off. Three players later someone makes a shot and they start choosing teams. Now I have to act especially composed because there are only ten people here over eleven years old and I'm one of them. It will just mean they don't want to play with anyone white if they pick one of the little kids instead of me, I say to myself. But I do get picked. When I ask who I'm supposed to cover they say "We're playing zone" so I stay back on the left on defense, since I'm one of the three tallest players on the team.

As soon as we get the ball on offense they pass it to me. I might have been able to drive but the band of little kids suddenly starts shooting near our basket. There are so many people around our basket it's like I'm seeing double. I'm afraid of hurting them so I give up the ball.

A couple of players on my team tell the little kids to get out of the way but they yell back, "We was here first." This argument goes on for the next ten baskets. These kids are stubborn and completely unintimidated. They swear and threaten to bring down their brothers and grandfathers. They also don't take the threats directed at them seriously, nor do they make the slightest effort to get out of the way except when one of our players drives to the basket, and then it's a minimal gesture, just enough to avoid a collision, like a matador foiling a bull.

Everyone on both teams is mad at the little kids now, but no one knows what to do about it because they're so small. Of course I don't say anything about it. I try to find it amusing. I say to myself,

Well, I've never seen five little kids intimidate ten men who want to play basketball before. I think of the different cities I've played playground basketball in and decide this is a real Philadelphia experience, but the truth is it's ruining my game. I'm still afraid of colliding with one of the little kids, so the few times I get the ball, I pass it after several tentative dribbles.

When the game is half over the little kids finally get off the court with the promise that they can play the winning team next game. A few plays later someone passes the ball to me and I shoot and miss everything. "Aaair baall" the little kids scream out in glee. They're watching everything from the sidelines. After that I don't shoot for the rest of the game, although I have a couple of opportunities. We lose by three baskets and I leave the court right away to avoid the embarrassment of not being picked for the next game.

I leave the park the same way I came, basically, passing the same people on their benches, although I don't look at them this time. I wonder vaguely whether the little kids got to play, but by the time I turn to look I'm too far away to tell who's playing and who isn't, or even how tall the people are who are shooting.

2

I got strangely depressed after the game. I guess I wanted to make a couple of baskets and hear them say "good hit" so I could play there again. I begin to walk slowly toward University City. It's funny, first I didn't want to leave my apartment and now I don't want to go back. I start walking up Baltimore Avenue and take a left on 40th Street, trying to shake off the effects of the game. All these row houses remind me of Somerville or of some lower middle-class suburb of New Jersey. It's hard for me to believe they're in the middle of a city as large as Philadelphia is supposed to be. I walk past Spruce and Locust onto Walnut. All kinds of vendors are out on the street selling stuff to the college kids. They're selling old color posters for a dollar of Elvis and Christie Brinkley and Prince. They're selling pretzels and pocketbooks and fruit and umbrellas, which is funny because there isn't a trace of a cloud in the sky. Next to a truck selling homemade Chinese food there's a truck selling

Italian ices. I walk over to the ice truck and ask the man for a medium-sized half-cherry, half-lemon.

The man in the truck, who weighs about seven hundred pounds, says, "No mixing unless you get a large."

"Okay, give me a medium lemon then." The thing is I used to go half and half on the medium-sized ices in New York all the time. In the summer I practically lived off the stuff, especially after I finished playing basketball. I loved beginning with the sweeter cherry and then finishing off with the more tart lemon. But still I decide I can't spring for a large ice when I used to get half and half on the mediums all the time, so I stick with the lemon and curse out the giant in the ice truck to myself.

The lemon isn't bad except that there's too much ice in it. It doesn't melt fast enough and actually sticks to the bottom of the cup, so I have to constantly tap the outside of the cup with my finger to dislodge it.

I decide I've had enough of University City, which I realize I'll be walking through hundreds of times this year anyway, so I head down a side street. I suddenly start thinking about getting a hooker. This makes me remember the way it works in various cities. In Hollywood it's all done by car. Since I didn't have one, I had a hard time convincing them I was for real. Even though I had a motel room a block or two away on Sunset Boulevard I'd often get rejected. They thought I was a cop, or they thought I was a pervert. Because I didn't have a car, they just didn't trust me.

From an intellectual point of view, the most interesting prostitutes are in New York. They'd often talk your ear off. They all have a story to tell. But I think I had my best times in the Combat Zone in Boston. Everything was so well organized there. When the cops were out on the street the hookers would go into the bars. I once walked into a bar and every woman in there was a prostitute. A lot of them were pretty too, and they were all hitting on me. I didn't know who to choose. It was like a scene in a Fellini movie.

I buy a newspaper and look at the porn movie ads so I'll know where to go and decide to take the subway on the Market Street line and ride till 13th Street. When I get off it's not even sunset yet so I'm not surprised that I don't see many women around. Still, I can tell there's not a concentrated area in Philadelphia like the Combat Zone or even like Hell's Kitchen in New York. It's diffuse, a couple here, a couple there. Also, all the good ones are walking with big black guys—their pimps, probably. But how do they expect to get business walking around with men?

I walk into a bar called The Fuel Pump, sit down and order a beer. I figure if I drink my beer slowly and then order another and drink that slowly it will be sunset when I leave, or maybe past sunset, and there'll be more women out then. I begin to wish I had some pot with me, but I have no idea how to get it in Philadelphia.

Someone turns on a TV and for the next fifteen minutes I watch a repeat of "Three's Company." Meanwhile, I look around the bar. Across from me are three white businessmen in suits. There are also a couple of black guys wearing sunglasses who may or may not be pimps, and two black women who may or may not be hookers. It's a small bar, and there's really only room for about ten people.

I start thinking about how I'd be better off in my apartment preparing for classes, except that by now I can teach these freshmen English classes in my sleep. Then I realize that I've almost run out of food and that I should do a big shopping at the Unimart before I go home. The thought of that store with all those chirpy students inside it depresses me, but I don't know where else to go in my neighborhood. While I'm thinking about this a woman comes over and sits next to me. She's either a very fair-skinned Negress or a swarthy white. In any event she's young, with high cheek bones and big light-green eyes, and she's quite pretty. I look down at my drink and see there's about a swallow of beer left. For a moment it gets quieter in the bar, or it feels quieter. Sometimes when I feel quiet like this I can hear everything in my body—all my blood traveling, all the cells with their individual messages moving across my nervous system.

Yikes, I'm losing it, I say to myself, so I start talking to the woman next to me who agrees that I can buy her a drink.

She says she's from Detroit and has only been in town for a month, but I'm not sure I believe her. Hookers are always saying they're new in town, although it could be true and I'm not completely sure that she's a hooker. For example, she's wearing a lot of makeup, but not that much makeup. I tell her I'm a teacher and the name of the school I teach at and that I just moved from California via New York and she nods and smiles and is politely encouraging but I don't think she really believes me. I mean if I'm a college English teacher what am I doing on a Saturday afternoon in a black bar looking for a prostitute?

Anyway, I make small talk with her and she tells me her name is Celeste. We talk about different cities for about five minutes. Slowly, people stop looking at us, as if they've accepted that we're an inevitability.

"So what are you doing these days?" I say. I'm finishing my second beer now and feeling a lot looser.

"Just trying to stay out of trouble."

"What's trouble?"

"Police are trouble. Hey, you're not a cop, are you?"

"No, I'm a teacher, just like I told you."

"Uh huh."

"So what did you do in Detroit, Celeste?"

I get a kick out of saying her name, which is almost certainly fake. I'm on my third beer now.

"I was a dancer."

Before I can get around to asking her if she's pursuing her dancing career in Philadelphia, she asks me if I want a date.

"Yes, I'd like that. Can you come back to my place? We can take a cab."

"What you wanna do?"

"Nothing special. What will it cost?"

We negotiate pretty quickly. It all goes surprisingly smoothly, even getting the cab, like it's destined to happen.

In the taxi Celeste asks me if I have anyone else back at my apartment and I say, "Nobody, just me."

"Not even one little girlfriend?" I shake my head no.

"How come a good looking guy like you don't have at least one girlfriend?"

I shrug my shoulders and say something nonchalantly about being new in town, but her compliment makes me feel good so I put my arm around her and tell her how these last years I've been moving a lot, and when I haven't been moving I've been afraid of moving.

I talk about this for a while and then I ask her about herself, being sure to tell her how pretty she is first. Celeste tells me that she's twenty-three years old, that she's "staying at different places right now," and that she graduated from high school with honors.

"I'm not ashamed to tell you that I graduated with honors" is the exact way she put it. Then she smiled and said, "You better watch it, I may end up in your class."

When we get out of the cab she asks me if I have any speed and tells me that she's really into the stuff. I tell her I'm sorry I don't and that I wish I had some pot and that if she'd like I'll buy her a bottle of something to drink. She shrugs her shoulders, it obviously doesn't mean much to her, but I was thinking as long as I'm near the Unimart I may as well get some shopping done.

About a half block from the store Celeste tugs at my arm. "I don't really care about the drink, don't do it on my account."

"It's okay. I have to get a few things anyway. Come on, it'll be fun. If we do it together it'll go by quickly."

We push on the glass door and see the store still full of college kids milling about as if they hadn't found their way out since the last time I saw them a week ago. They're wearing their school T-shirts and sweatshirts and a lot of them are wearing shorts, especially the girls.

As I start to go down the cookie aisle I put my arm around Celeste. When I was younger I always loved walking around with a pretty woman but I thought it was immature to feel that way. But now that I'm over thirty and almost too old to play basketball I enjoy it more than ever. It's amazing how much credibility you get and how much less intimidating the world seems just because you're walking with someone good-looking. People make way for you and gaze at you seriously and almost everything suddenly becomes easier. For example, normally I might be paralyzed for a half hour trying to figure out what kind of TV dinner to get or what kind of candy. But now I make my choices swiftly and definitively and put each item in the food cart Celeste is pushing beside me. I get a turkey TV dinner, a beef TV dinner, a can of minestrone, two cans of ravioli, a six-pack of Country Time Lemonade, a big Mr. Goodbar, some Nacho Cheese Doritos, three apples, a box of Pepperidge Farm Sugar Cookies, a loaf of Wonder Bread, and a half pound of salami. Celeste looks so cute pushing the food cart along that I decide I'll buy her a bottle of champagne at the liquor store around the corner after we finish at the Unimart.

Even standing in the line at the cash register turns out to be fun. There's a football player standing right behind us, wearing number 88, holding hands with a mousy blonde wearing a new pair of Calvin Kleins. When he looks at Celeste in her short black leather skirt his jaw nearly drops. I can't resist looking at 88 once more just before we leave the store, and sure enough he's still staring at us.

. . . I remember I was in a good mood all the way back, I might even have been whistling as I climbed up the three flights with Celeste. I started putting the food away, not in any particular order, just in the right bins in the refrigerator, but I left out the champagne and the sugar cookies on my kitchen table.

"Hey Mister, could you take care of me now?" Celeste said as she walked into the kitchen. The "Mister" kind of threw me but I didn't show it. I said "sure" and gave her the money I promised her back in the bar. She counted it and then put it inside her sock. I hadn't even noticed she was wearing socks, they were so small and transparent.

"You wanna get comfortable now," she says.

"I'm very comfortable."

"Where you want to do it, then, here in the kitchen?"

"Why don't we have some champagne first to celebrate our shopping?"

"Mister, I don't usually spend this much time. I've got to get back to take care of business, you know?"

I start to feel a little foolish, but then I get another idea.

"Why don't we call it a night," I say very evenly but decisively, like a judge.

"You don't want nothing from me?"

"No, no. I've had a lot of fun with you already. I'd like to get your phone number though."

She opens her purse and writes it in lipstick on a piece of stationery I had lying around from the last school I taught at in Santa Barbara. I stare at it for a few seconds and ask her if it's her real number and she laughs and says, "Of course it is."

"When can I call you? When is it best to reach you?"

"I'm usually in by midnight."

Then just as she's about to go out the door I tell her to wait and I go back to the kitchen and give her the bottle of champagne.

"For you," I say.

She smiles again and thanks me. "That's real sweet of you," is what she says. Then she tells me to call her anytime.

. . . As soon as she leaves I press my head to the door and listen to her steps as she goes downstairs until I can't hear them anymore. Then it gets quiet and I worry about hearing my blood again, so I go in my bedroom and turn on the TV. But the show doesn't hold my attention and I shut it off after a few minutes and get a beer instead.

. . . Now it's dark. I'm lying in bed sipping my beer, remembering the basketball game, The Fuel Pump, remembering and thinking about everything. My idea about getting her phone number was that now that I've established some kind of credit with Celeste she might agree to meet me and walk to school with me, just for my first day of classes. Let the kids see that their freshman comp teacher has a really hip-looking girlfriend. Let them see that before I even open my mouth and say a word to them. It would be a good investment in my career.

From outside I hear a scream on the streets and then the sound of car tires screeching. It's unclear whether the car is screeching to a halt or else screeching as it speeds away, but either way I don't let it disturb me. I have such a vivid picture of walking into class with my arm around Celeste that I can almost blend into it the way a very light cloud, if you squint your eyes a little, can blend into the sky. I don't want to let the picture go. Not for a while anyway. I don't even want to go to sleep.

The Opposite Girl

The thing about me is I always did the opposite of what people expected. Even as a kid, instead of dolls or playing games with girls I read travel books and played hide and seek with the boy across the street. Needless to say, my parents, despite thinking of themselves as great individualists, always considered me a queer fish. For instance, they liked to take the family to see the Dodgers. My brother and sister would really get into it, but I used to wander off to the concession stands and talk to the vendors. When my father asked my why, I told him the vendors were doing things too and I'd rather watch them than the ballplayers. He smiled, but he also had this funny look in his eyes like I might be an alien. He was a hippie in the '60s and my mother, who basically follows everything he says, used to be one too. He liked to say he raised his kids according to a theory of giving them the maximum amount of freedom possible. It always sounded like a rationalization for not being much of a father to me, but I guess it worked for my brother and sister who get along fine with him, as far as I can tell.

When high school ended I told my father I was moving to New York, that I'd support myself waitressing and wouldn't bug him about money. He said, "What about college?" and I said, "What about it?" "You're a very bright girl," he said, and I smiled for a second but then shrugged and said, "If I want to go I'll get a scholarship or work my way through but I won't take any money from you." He argued mildly before giving in (he liked thinking of himself as a real mild dude), and of course my mother gave in too.

Then right before I left he handed me a few hundred dollars in traveler's checks.

Just seeing New York and walking around in it was an incredible rush. I stayed in a "hotel" in the East Village at first and got a job as a waitress in a place called Amoebas near the Bowery. Right away I started making friends with people in the downtown performance/ dance scene. Every day I seemed to have amazing adventures. One of my friends, a choreographer named Miodini, and her boyfriend, a very sweet black dancer named Taylor, taught me how to live in a car. A couple of weeks later I left my room, bought a truly old Chevy and lived in it for three months. Nothing bad ever happened (I knew where to park it at night), plus I saved rent, met a lot of interesting men, a number of whom became lovers, and learned a lot about New York.

I stopped living in the car when it got really cold and just too difficult. At first I crashed with Miodini, but she was having this intense thing with her new lover from Brazil and between that and her primal (scream) therapy—it was too loud to get much sleep there. I must have had over fifteen roommates in the next year, mostly between Avenues A and E. They were quite an assortment— painters, punks, bikers, tattoo freaks, etc. After a while I had to write my parents to tell them to contact me care of Amoebas because no mail was reaching me. I could picture my father reading that and smiling quizzically as he told my mother, or maybe raising an eyebrow, which would be high emotion for him. Anyway, I knew he'd say something, and sure enough in his next letter he wrote, "We'd like it if you had an address"— strong words for the mild-mannered man!

Just as my father was freaking out, albeit on his own very low frequency, I met these great German jazz musicians named Peter and Gunther at a party in Tribecca. Immediately we became friends and got along so well it was really unbelievable. There was never anything sexual between me and either one of them (in fact, it turned out they were a couple), but I'd never been able to communicate on such a deep level with any guys before so I ended up staying in their loft on North Moore Street for over a year. In exchange for rent I did some cooking and cleaning for them, which I really didn't mind, plus some secretarial work. (I kind of became their business manager.) Meanwhile, my father was appeased and knew where to call me on Christmas or whatever.

I won't say it was a perfect arrangement, and there were certainly times when I felt excluded, but all things considered it was a pretty happy year. The only thing that was sad was their careers didn't pan out and they decided to try to get studio work in L.A. They even asked me to go with them but I had to say no. They were practically in tears when they said goodbye to me. Peter and Gunther—I still write to them—they were incredible!

For some time things downtown had been getting weird. Miodini was in South America with her new boyfriend and no one knew where Taylor was. Everywhere I went people were talking about AIDS and I started thinking that maybe I should check out another part of the city. Fortunately I can type well and I'm pretty good-looking so I was able to get a job as a receptionist/secretary at Columbia Law School. It was a real zero job—lots of unwelcome flirting by the professors—but it paid better than anything I'd ever had and I was able to move into a two-bedroom apartment, with this very straight schoolteacher named Norma, on the Upper West Side.

Right after I moved I realized that people uptown were talking about AIDS too. So disease obsessed, eternally puritanical America strikes again, I said to myself. Anyway, I certainly wasn't going to be like everyone else and let a virus that was afflicting less than 1 percent of the population control my life. One of the things Miodini used to say was that the only force stronger than sexual hysteria in America was antisexual hysteria, the forces, never too far away, that could always be used as reasons not to have sex. Now that "safe sex" was a buzzword, all I could think of was if people were so scared why bother to do it at all? Men could stay home and use their socks and women could buy zucchinis. When I talked to Norma like that she used to get pissed and tell me I was being really irresponsible. She said she wouldn't dream of sleeping with more than one person now, plus this one person would *have* to be monogamous.

So I wasn't surprised really when she started shacking up with one of her fellow teachers about a year ago. It was just as well, in a way, since it left me the apartment almost completely to myself. It was the first time I'd ever been alone in an apartment and I was looking forward to it. I wanted to meet new friends and maybe get into dancing and I needed the energy boost that being alone can give you.

I'm pretty sure it began with this feeling of having extra energy, which somehow got transformed into a heightened awareness of my apartment. What I mean is, without really knowing it my senses sharpened and my sensitivity to my environment increased about tenfold. At night I'd hear noises I never knew existed before, and I'd smell things too, as if my nose were on special patrol to detect gas from the oven, for example, which I might have left on. It's funny how once your range of sense perception increases it expands indefinitely, as if self-doubt were the only thing that ever held it back. In other words, once I discovered that the noises I was hearing in the building were really happening, by rushing to the kitchen to shut off the faucet or looking out the peephole to see a neighbor actually opening his door across the hall I began thinking (at times) that I could hear everything—even the path the cockroaches were making across the kitchen counters.

When I walked outside now I sensed all the anxiety in people's faces that I'd never seen before. And when I thought about people in my past, for instance, Peter and Gunther, I realized they'd had it too, that I'd just never been aware of it before. In general my whole being felt on alert and I suddenly became starved for information. I started reading the papers every day, sometimes three different ones, and watching the news at night on Norma's TV. There was the usual quota of murders and disasters, but since I hadn't paid attention before, they scared me, especially this Gary Heidnik guy in Philadelphia who seduced and tortured all those mentally retarded women. News coverage of AIDS was everywhere, of course. Apparently it was increasing more than anyone imagined. The whole idea of a virus of unknown origin being sexually transmitted and slowly destroying people seemed out of a twisted Japanese—no, make that German—sci-fi movie, but that's what the news said was happening.

One night I started thinking back on all my lovers. I was pretty sure none of them had ever slept with men or had shot up drugs, but how could I be sure? Being told wasn't being sure, and since I hadn't really asked, I didn't even have the reassurance of being told. Also,

the latency period of the virus, or the fact that you could transmit it
without even knowing you had it, all of that was hard to deal with.
I even occasionally wondered if I could have somehow gotten it
while I was living with Peter and Gunther, from a glass I drank out
of or a teaspoon or something.

I started calling the AIDS hotline a lot, sometimes two or three
times a day. As soon as they'd answer one question I'd think of three
more. It was ridiculous in a way. I was pretty freaked about it but
eventually I went in and got tested. Of course the results were
negative (I somehow knew they would be), and of course the dikey-
looking nurse there gave me the standard lecture about safe sex, but
I'd already decided to give up sex for a while. It was just too
nerve-racking. This was about a half a year ago.

Well, okay, now that I was celibate I decided to organize my time
in different ways and I immediately joined a modern dance class. So
what happens? My teacher, Gary, turns out to be this incredible-
looking, very charismatic, outrageously gifted dancer. At night,
when I'd start hearing the noises in the building, the only thing that
could calm me down was thinking about him. I called Norma and
said, "What am I going to do, I've got a wicked crush on my dance
teacher?"

"Does he know it?"

"I don't know."

"Why don't you ask him out for a drink after class?"

I decided Norma was right and went to the bathroom to check my
makeup. I forgot to say that I'd been spending a lot of time and
money on makeup. I had twenty-six different kinds of lipstick, thirty
different shades of eyeshadow, and eight different kinds of blush. It
was like an infinitely challenging puzzle, trying to coordinate everything to get the best possible results. But it was frustrating too,
since I'd never feel I had it right and would end up doing my face
completely over five or ten times a day, even during my lunch break
at Columbia.

Maybe Gary was too amazing-looking and too charismatic.
Whatever it was I still couldn't bring myself to ask him. I started
calling Norma for advice again and she began giving me pep talks.
I discovered that between 4:00 and 4:30 she'd be home from school

before her boyfriend got back and I'd call her then for fifteen minutes every day. Finally she said I had to stop calling her about it, that I just had to ask him out or she'd stop talking to me.

As usual Norma made sense, but at the end of my next class a number of students (mostly men) sort of surrounded Gary and I just couldn't talk to him out of the teacher/student mode. When I got home I did my makeup again, experimenting with a new eyeliner and skin base and trying to work them into the puzzle. It was seven o'clock when I stopped—I'd been doing it for two straight hours. I felt so weirded out about it that I started to cry. Then I reached for the phone and for some reason called my father at work. It was a few minutes past four in California.

He seemed pretty glad to hear from me, in his eternally low-key way. Of course I didn't explain to him about Gary or my makeup or being "on alert" or any of the other things I'd been preoccupied with. At the end of the conversation I asked him if I could call him tomorrow at the same time, and he said sure and that he would call me. I said no, that it would be better for me to call him. (I didn't want him spending any money on it since it was my idea. Also, it didn't seem fair since I'd only been calling him at Christmas or birthdays, and one year I just sent postcards and barely called at all.)

Anyway, I called my father four more days in a row, at seven o'clock, and we talked a little. I asked him about my mom and my brother and sister. He asked me about New York and my job. It wasn't a big deal but it wasn't bad either. Then the last time he had this familiar-sounding critical tone in his voice and he started asking me how I could afford to call him like this if everything was all right. I told him I was fine and got off the phone a minute later.

I stayed in that weekend and didn't call anyone. Instead, I did a lot of makeup and watched TV and didn't sleep much. On Monday morning (this is about five days ago) I called in sick at work, then walked into the kitchen and drank a couple of Scotches straight up. I began reading a postcard I'd gotten from an ex-lover who was in Boston now, and thinking about how ballsy I was with this guy when I lived in my car, I suddenly called Gary at his studio.

On the phone his voice sounded soft and distant and he laughed nervously, almost as much as I did. I finally said straight out that we should get together for a drink and he suggested Thursday at 6:00 at The West End (which was nice of him since that was much nearer me than his studio), and just like that I had a date with him. I let out a little scream when the call was over, like I sometimes do during sex, and ran out on the street deliriously happy. A throng of people were out, as usual: Cubans, blacks, Puerto Ricans, Chinese, they all passed me on the sidewalk. I didn't see anxiety or fear on their faces this time, just this kind of special concentration as they all moved through space together. It was like a vindication of New York, of my decision to live here at the true center of human life. But then I started worrying that someone from the law school might see me since I was only a few blocks from Columbia, so I went back to my apartment.

It was hard waiting for my date and I began to worry about a lot of things. I decided that my long but otherwise very average straight brown hair had to be fixed—but how? I thought about cutting it various ways till I thought I'd go blind from visualizing all the possibilities. Finally I went out and bought two wigs. Wig One had darker hair, which I thought might highlight the green in my eyes; Wig Two was blonde, which I thought might make me look a little more glamorous in general. In the end, I decided against both of them.

At night I'd lie still, trying to sleep, my senses getting sharper and sharper till I'd hear the footsteps in the hallway or the cockroaches in the kitchen again. Then, like pushing a new channel on TV, I'd start thinking about Gary. He was blond and blue-eyed with unusually broad shoulders for a dancer. Come to think of it he looked pretty Californian, even a little like my father, though he was much more charismatic, of course. I started wondering if he'd expect to go to bed on our first date, which might be a problem since I hadn't done it in so long. I'd probably be pretty awkward just from being out of practice, and if I were that awkward everything might fall apart on the first night. Before my celibacy I'd never realized the insecurities you can have after you stop having sex regularly. I knew there'd be physical frustration, of course, but I didn't anticipate how it eats away at your very sense of yourself. I actually toyed with the idea of calling someone from work or even going to a bar (armed with a sheaf of condoms, of course) just to get in some practice.

When that got to be too tempting, I'd get up and do some makeup and just hope things would be okay.

The night of the date we were both on time. The West End is one of those places that's fairly dark but lively at the same time. There's a juke box and a number of video games that are both usually on and a self-service cafeteria on one side of the bar. We took a table just under a giant TV that jutted out about ten feet from the wall.

Gary was wearing a brown tweed sports jacket that showed off his shoulders. I wore a light pink jumper and a lot of pink makeup with baby blue eyeshadow. He looked very cute and was making a real effort to be nice, I thought, but it was funny, away from his studio he wasn't so imposing. He seemed a little inexperienced, actually, especially when we ordered. It's strange how that happens, but the same thing happened to me. My studio used to be downtown in my Chevy, then it was the North Moore loft, I guess. But I didn't really have a studio now and Gary didn't seem to have one either. I excused myself from the table and went into the ladies' room and checked my makeup. God, I'm starting to nitpick this guy out of existence, I thought to myself.

After we had a couple of drinks we both started to relax. I told him stories about my life downtown, without getting too specific, of course, and he laughed a lot. We had hamburgers for dinner—not very romantic food, but tasty. When we started walking down Broadway, he put his arm around me and I liked it and felt attracted to him again. He asked me if he could walk me home and I said yes. I could feel myself getting really excited but couldn't help remembering all those gay-looking guys crowding around him in the studio. I have to admit I still had some questions about him and worried what I would do if he put a move on me.

A block from my apartment we stopped and he mentioned that I must have a nice view of the river. We talked about the goddamn Hudson River for about five minutes. Then he took my hand and asked if he could come in with me.

"I don't think so," I said, "my place is a mess and I'm real tired." My heart was beating about a million miles an hour.

"Well," he said, shrugging his shoulders and smiling a little sadly, "I've enjoyed it."

"Me too," I said, thinking he was gorgeous but ineffectual. Then before I could prepare myself he stepped forward like a baseball player moving into the batter's box and gave me a fairly hard eighth-grade-type closed-mouth kiss on the lips.

"Goodnight," he said, turning away and waving at me. "See you in the studio." I don't know if I said goodnight or not. I think I probably played it pretty straight and waved and everything until I got to the elevator, where I closed my eyes and felt myself get dizzy and wondered if I were going to throw up. Then when I realized I wasn't I started seeing his kiss over and over like on an instant replay. Each time I tried to freeze the moment of contact to see if his tongue actually got inside my lips but I could never freeze it in time to tell.

When I got back to my apartment I ran to the bathroom looking for some kind of disinfectant but all I could see was lipstick and eyeshadow. With one swipe I cleared my sink of all my lipsticks. While they clattered to the floor I looked at my eyeshadow and moisturizers and screamed at them, "You bastards just killed me!" Then I ran to the kitchen and started opening and closing cabinets at random. Finally I picked up a can of Ajax from under the sink and ran back to the bathroom and poured it on a wet facecloth and washed my lips, inside and out, very thoroughly, plus my tongue. Meanwhile I was grinding some plastic lipstick containers under my feet. When they snapped they sounded like water bugs being killed.

When I stopped washing I realized I was nauseated, and sure enough, five minutes later I threw up. I don't know if it was because of the Ajax or what but it was pretty violent. Then I just lay down and cried and sort of half slept for a couple of hours, which takes me pretty much up to the present.

What I want to know now is, how justified are my fears? Does objective reality justify them or are my reactions more subjective than I realize? Also, how do you even split yourself up into objective and subjective compartments to be able to judge? I thought of calling Norma but threw that out and ended up calling my father. My mother answered instead and didn't act all that surprised that I'd called. First she asked me a few questions, which I mostly answered with one word, then she said "Would you like to speak to your father?"

"Yes," I said.

He started off in his typical quiet style, even telling me an anecdote about his office party, as if I gave a flying one. In the middle of his dopey monologue I just blurted out about coming back from a basically innocent, disappointing date and getting a crummy goodnight kiss and washing my mouth out with Ajax because I was afraid of getting AIDS and how I used to be so brave three years ago when I got here and now I was just the opposite and was feeling scared of everything.

There was this deadly silence for a while until he asked me a couple of questions about my life in New York. Then I heard his voice waver a little (Why is everyone such a coward, I thought) until he finally said, "I'd like to come see you in New York. Will you see me if I come?"

I told him yes and hung up the phone a minute later. I have to admit I felt a strange kind of rush. I looked around my apartment and everything was quiet and beautifully bright. It looked like it does when it's snowed overnight without your knowing it and everything you see in the morning is shiny and still. Except that it was really better than that. In its own way it was better than anything I'd ever felt.

Mason

From his favorite bench by the bocci courts he watched the old men and women leave the beach in unison, their hairless white legs in slow and furious motion as they tried to get inside before the storm. Then he got up with exaggerated slowness, as if to ridicule their sense of panic, and began to walk leisurely past the emergency medical services truck that was lurking behind a group of palm trees. He walked past Dr. MacBain's outlandishly pink house and down Clinton Street, with its mostly small white houses separated from each other only by a palm tree or two or by an arrangement of flowers. Halfway down the street was the inn Mrs. Ash owned (she'd started it with the not quite enough money her husband left her), where on days when he wanted to feel dignified he reminded himself that she always decorously, softly, but with a hint of insistence called him "the Manager." Since the full-time staff consisted of only two, he was often forced to call himself a handyman as well. He did that kind of work, after all: plumbing and gardening, mowing the lawn, cleaning the pool, walking Mrs. Ash's Doberman. He knew his skills were limited, but that didn't prevent him from occasionally enjoying with Mrs. Ash the fiction that they were not, in return for which he allowed her to pretend that the inn had a viable future, which he knew it didn't. Its demise was as imminent as that of its few elderly inhabitants, who couldn't afford St. Petersburg any longer and had drifted over to Gulfport. There they found a kind of satisfaction in the rhythm of tropical rain and checkers and languor-

ous swings on the beach and the harmless birds squawking at the
end of the street with no one under sixty in sight.

He was thirty years younger than most people in Gulfport and he
was wondering again what he was doing here and worse still why he
hadn't wondered more about it before. His least-favorite feeling was
of having made a fundamental mistake in judgment, yet here he was
in this mausoleum, this floating crypt. It wasn't exactly as if he were
in love with old people, extreme heat, or tiny towns, so what was he
doing in Gulfport when he could be living with people his own age
in a real city like Miami or New Orleans?

The thing is, he thought he'd had a good plan. After he collected
the money for his accident he'd quit the company where he was
night watchman and drove south from Wilmington. He'd always
wanted to see what living in Florida would be like and thought
Tampa would be a good place to start since it was in the middle of
the state and had a pro football team (with pro basketball maybe just
around the corner). But it was more expensive than he'd thought and
he ended up in Gulfport, a town that was little more than a bay, the
beach, and a few streets. The town, of course, would never of itself
have been enough to make him stay. Ultimately he stayed because he
began to listen to Mrs. Ash, although she had not fooled him at first
either. When he met her he thought, Pretty woman—too bad she's
pushing fifty (he now thought she was nearer sixty). She also struck
him as one of those melodramatic widows who are always in heat
but will never do anything about it. He knew that and yet he let her
talk him into working for her, so that the inn that housed him when
he first arrived became his place of work and his former hostess
became his employer. The town merely stayed the calm and anonymous backdrop for Mrs. Ash's monologues, most of which dealt
with her husband, who apparently had been the most noble high
school English teacher in the history of central Florida. He would
listen to her marathon evocations of him, tales of his unrewarded
acts of kindness in the community, his perfect attendance record at
Central High until the day of his fatal coronary, his "impeccable
decorum and gentlemanliness" in all things concerning her. He
himself had had a mother (now also dead) who raved on like that,
about anything she could attach her emotions to, be it the weather,

television, or the occasional articles she read in *Reader's Digest,* so he felt he understood about her talking.

He did wonder about her nocturnal visits, or rather his visits to her room which she requested once every week or two. She was inexhaustible in her capacity to think of some pretext for him to be summoned to her room, where she'd keep him at least an hour, whispering her monologues which eventually included questions about him. It was not only these nighttime conversations (where she spoke from her bed with her head propped up by three pillows and he stood with his hand on the doorknob) that made him suspicious but the sudden burst of favors she'd do for him: the tie she bought him, the times she'd do his laundry, the unasked-for raises, the musical hush she would greet him with, and then the strange flow of delicate perspiration that accompanied it all.

Worst of all were her questions. She said she wanted to know everything she could about what she called his "unfortunate career reversals." He'd told her that his first good job was at a detective agency in Boston.

"That must have been terribly stressful," she said, leaning forward in her bed and turning the fan from high to low to hear him better.

"The stress was okay, it was my boss who was the problem. He crossed me, so I quit."

Unbeknownst to him, his hand was caressing the doorknob. Mrs. Ash noticed and asked him if he wanted to leave but he lied and said he didn't. Then he had to tell her about working for the insurance company, investigating accident claims. He told her that he didn't like jerking people around for a company that was crooked, so he'd had to quit that too. Mrs. Ash uttered a strange cooing sound and placed her hand on one of her ample bosoms as if she were wounded. Finally he had to tell her about his job as night watchman. As he expected she made a big deal out of how dangerous it was to protect a company at night.

"I had no problem about that. Being protected *from* the company was what my problem was."

He went on to explain about the faulty structure of the stairway that collapsed under him. After the company settled with him for the accident he figured he'd leave a winner, so he quit. (He didn't tell her that his attorney had wanted to sue for four times as much.)

All her personal questions unnerved him, but he put up with them because he thought she was a kind enough woman and it would be nice to pick up a few dollars while he got his bearings at the inn. Another reason it was not more irritating was Lorraine, whom he met at the Bay Bar a week after he started working for Mrs. Ash. She was a broad-shouldered woman with a pretty smile, in her early forties (his age), who worked a roulette table at the Gulfport Casino across the street. One night her car broke down and he gave her a lift to Tampa. She had an easy way about her and it seemed to cost her nothing to ask him up to her room. But once it came down to actual sex she was too resistant, which made it hard and then eventually impossible to do anything. He never called her or went into the Bay Bar again. Two weeks later he sold his car, telling Mrs. Ash he needed some extra cash.

After Lorraine he did very little about women. The first few months he went into Tampa once every week or two and then once a month looking for hookers, until without remembering when he gave it up. Occasionally he would walk down to the store that sold candy and *People* magazine, but they didn't carry *Penthouse* or *Playboy* so he felt he was slowly forgetting what women looked like. Gulfport became a slow, steady pool of confusion where one's sex could easily sink like a harmless stone, where everyone circulated or sat on their pool rocks in a silence they no longer had to will, until their ages were forgotten, their genders as confused as so many specks of sand.

At the beginning of 58th Street his chain of memories stopped abruptly. He could see Mrs. Ash waving and calling out to him. Though he couldn't hear her precise words he knew it was just his name, Mason, that she said and that what she was waving like a handkerchief was a letter he'd received. That didn't make him walk any faster. For some time his mail had consisted of nothing but bills, but for Mrs. Ash the delivery of his mail was an event that had acquired a faintly transcendent quality. She was still waving the letter when he got within ten feet of her, and he could see her nervous blue eyes darting uncomfortably in their fixtures.

"Mason, this came for you."

She was wearing a flowered, pale green dress—the approximate color of the Gulfport Casino. He took the envelope, noticing a thin line of perspiration at the top of her forehead, thanked her, and bowed slightly to give this ritual the formal touch he knew she wanted. As soon as he excused himself, however, he cursed himself for bothering to do this. When he got to the door he could see her reflected in the glass. She had turned around to watch him and he felt he could still smell a trace of the body lotion she used to try to camouflage her perspiration.

Once inside he waved to Corpse C, who was just emerging from the downstairs bathroom. Corpse C, whose actual name was Floyd Carruthers, was a bachelor in his mid-seventies who suffered from arthritis and chronic constipation and had a lung problem that led to occasional coughing fits. Moreover, his face was disfigured by liver spots that reminded Mason of the black blotches on overripe bananas.

Mason knew the names of all the tenants, but he preferred his lettering system (Corpse A, Corpse B, Corpse C, etc.) as a way of keeping his distance. Once Mrs. Ash had suggested that he could make some money if he wanted to assist the physical therapist who visited twice a week. "No thanks," he'd said curtly. When she pressed him about it he said, "No way I'm getting involved with corpse maintenance."

"Why do you call them that?" she'd asked, her gaze at once tragic and compassionate, an expression she often had when she discussed her husband. Mason's heart skipped a beat. Although he'd liked thinking and, to a degree, even talking brutally about the old people at the inn, he actually liked many of them and pitied all of them more than he could say.

"It's what they are, walking corpses. This whole town is nothing but a concentration camp for old people."

. . . On the way upstairs now, holding his envelope, he waved to Corpse E. With some difficulty Corpse E, who was spastic, waved back. Then Mason opened the envelope and found a phone bill from Wilmington which he'd already paid.

In his room he began to search through the papers on his desk. It took him a good deal longer than he wanted to find the correct place in his files for the phone bill. The first few months he'd been quite meticulous about organizing his correspondence, but as the letters from Delaware diminished, the time and space he afforded them on his desk were replaced by paperback books he checked out of the Gulfport library (or sometimes bought), all of which, from *Robinson Crusoe* to *Huckleberry Finn,* dealt with escape of one kind or another. He had over thirty such books. He picked up *Robinson Crusoe* and began to leaf through the pages when he suddenly stopped. The sun came in obliquely through the blinds and he moved nearer his fan and stayed still for a few minutes thinking of nothing except that the storm hadn't come. His white chinos were the color of the sun.

So the old idiots ran like cattle for nothing, there wasn't even a drop of rain, he thought. Then he moved away from the fan to the door and, looking once to be sure none of the corpses were watching him, went downstairs to find Mrs. Ash. Halfway down the stairs he saw the top of her head in profile. She was sitting in the rocking chair, so still it didn't stir and knitting furiously at the perpetually revised and unnecessary white cotton sweater that he knew she was making for him.

"Do we have food for tonight?" she asked, in what for her was a matter-of-fact voice but for someone else would seem hushed and breathless.

"We have enough," he said, without expression. He was looking down directly at her head, like a billiard player preparing a shot, and he could see her network of hair—tangled and streaked with black dye. He didn't feel repulsion, but he couldn't kill his small, persistent anger when he *felt* (felt even more than he saw) the drops of perspiration in her hair, on her back, her thighs, and in the useless center of her sexuality.

He went downstairs automatically. These midday talks with her were such a feature of his daily life they no longer seemed dreamlike. He would sit leaning forward slightly, like a jockey, in the wicker chair directly in front of her, five feet away. She wouldn't look up from her knitting. The tips of the needles were gleaming in the sunlight. He watched them for a moment, no longer certain if he were somehow sitting there two weeks ago and wondering to himself if the same conversation that took place then would recur now.

"Mason, I'd like to speak to you for a moment before you go out. Is that possible?"

"Of course," he said, not without some irony.

"You may remember that last week I made you a business proposal."

"I remember." It was an offer of a partnership whereby he would pay for his percentage of the inn through work instead of money. It was, Mason realized, a clear bribe to make him stay longer, and he'd turned her down cold.

"I wonder if you've thought about reconsidering."

"I don't reconsider. I try to get things right the first time."

A little sigh escaped from her slightly parted lips but it didn't interrupt the rhythm of her knitting, which stayed as steady as time itself.

"Perhaps if you'd tell me your principle objection we could discuss it."

"My principle objection is that if you become part owner of a place you're making a commitment and I don't exactly feature myself spending a big part of my future at this inn or in this town."

"My, you can be a very sarcastic man, Mason. Did you know that in our entire marriage I can't recall one occasion when Mr. Ash was ever sarcastic with me?"

"Like I keep telling you, we're two different people."

"Well, I won't keep you any longer. I don't think you feel like talking to me very much this afternoon."

She stopped knitting. Her cheeks had turned a red so vivid that, although he had seen it before, it amazed him. He looked down at the rug. In the distance he could hear the hopeless rhythm of Corpse C's cough and spit. He wanted to leave but couldn't. Instead he said, "You know I enjoy talking to you."

"Do you? I sometimes think there isn't enough . . . variety in my conversation, that it must get tiresome."

"No."

"For you?"

"No."

"Well, you're being polite."

He said nothing. There were actually no thoughts in him at all, merely a recognition that he was being sucked into the soft hum of her monologue again—the repetitive yap about everything and nothing with which she filled her time with him and which accompanied her knitting like a metronome.

A half hour later he mumbled an ''excuse me'' and rose from his chair, careful to avoid her eyes as he walked out to the porch, wondering how much he had offended her. From the porch he turned around and saw the back of her matted-down hair through the window. Then she turned to watch him and he turned away with only a split second of eye contact between them.

He looked up at the late afternoon sun. The sun wasn't solid, it was more like a broken egg, except that the running yellow had congealed in a horseshoe shape around the trees. He kept a close watch on it to avoid her gaze and to ultimately force her back to her knitting. In front of him two female corpses were sitting in rocking chairs, chatting about the need for rain. He looked at the lawn he had cut that morning. In the distance two male corpses (B and D) were looking for a shuttlecock and clutching their badminton rackets tightly.

He decided he would not even try to pretend to clean the pool. Instead he began walking down Clinton Street toward the beach. He didn't understand himself why he was so angry until he reached Dr. MacBain's house, from where the beach was first visible. She had wanted to talk about her husband again, he had sensed another tidal wave of tributes coming, but he had cut her off and had been sarcastic doing it. That would be all right except he felt guilty as soon as he did it and thus bound to make it up to her. Result: thirty more minutes of his rapidly diminishing life devoted to her memories of The Great Man. Even that would be all right if his listening to her hymns of praise for him were an occasional act of kindness instead of a regular part of his life, and even that would be all right if he had a woman of his own or even Mrs. Ash herself. But he knew she would never sleep with him. She would bribe him into staying with partnership plans, she would cook and knit and shop for him, but she couldn't violate her husband's spirit, which sleeping with him or any other man would do. Meanwhile she was getting more possessive than ever. A month ago, when there'd finally been a single female guest under sixty (a stringy-haired, bird-faced librarian on her way to a library convention), Mrs. Ash fairly devoured her with cross-examination, competing with her relentlessly in what she liked to call "the art of conversation." She also seemed to wear a new outfit every time she confronted her rival, each one more elaborate and frilly than the last. Of course, she started questioning him too. The summonses to her room increased and she would try with pathetic transparency to discover his impressions of the librarian, who was so nondescript that she seemed like a distant memory before she even left.

It was during one of these interrogations that he thought she asked him to rub her neck, this request coming after she described her husband's prowess "in the art of massage." He pretended he didn't hear her but when he left her room he had an erection that wouldn't go away. Remembering this now he hated her and vowed again that he would leave.

That she pretended to be so proper when she lusted for him, that she invoked her husband's name like a God when she yearned to betray that God—and at her age, when she was almost old enough to be his mother.

He crossed the street and headed automatically toward his bench. There were very few people on the beach. It was as if once they left because of the imagined storm they believed it had really come and ruined the day.

He saw them as soon as he sat down—only ten feet from him, midway between his bench and the last bocci court. But he let a minute pass before he picked them up, first because it was so improbable that it seemed like a hallucination and then because it somehow seemed forbidden. There were three wrinkled, color pages, bleached from too much sun, of a naked woman, pulled out from a men's magazine. Her name was Victoria and she was posing on top of a sailboat, a horse, a racing car, and an airplane. The blurb printed under her pictures revealed, "She likes sports, travel, and excitement—'anything that moves excites me,' says Vicki."

He stared at the pictures a full fifteen minutes, reading the printed accompaniment four or five times. Then he folded the pages carefully, put them in his back pocket, and headed back to the inn. He had already decided he would leave, but he was still angry anyway. To have spent so many hundreds of hours listening to an old foolish widow, wondering if she wanted to sleep with him, wondering if he hated her, wondering about her at all, while he let all traces of young women's flesh, real flesh, desert him, so that the pictures of Vicki were his first images of it in months—that was insanity, an insanely slow suicide. It was a problem he should have spent a day or two on and instead it had taken a year.

After dinner he spread the pictures out on his bed so he could see all of them simultaneously. There was one of Vicki on a sailboat (her rear end arched up into the sky, as big as the sun) that was so beautiful it shocked him. When he heard Mrs. Ash start to come upstairs he gathered up the pictures. It was incredible that he'd found them on the beach. He felt like Robinson Crusoe when he saw Friday's footprint, and looking lovingly at his favorite book he decided to temporarily put the pictures inside it. He also decided then to go to sleep early so he'd have plenty of time to pack in the morning. He would make his explanation to Mrs. Ash as brief as possible, and possibly he would make none at all.

But after half an hour of trying he was still unable to sleep, alternately blaming his weak fan and a persistent mosquito he couldn't kill. He expected to be haunted by the pictures of Vicki, but instead he envisioned Mrs. Ash, her gestures and positions as she talked to him from the rocking chair, or in the front yard holding his letter.

Usually when he saw her in his mind at night he was able to use the steady noise of the fan to concentrate on and dissolve the images. Tonight, though, he couldn't rid himself of her in her pale green casino-colored dress (the reflection he saw in the window that afternoon) or her arms waving to him in the sun. She was over fifty but her body was young. It was a strange joke of nature, but there it was—her body had few wrinkles or sags and it was still lush like a young bride's, as if she had stopped its cells' normal progression of decay as soon as she found out she would never sleep with her husband again, nor with any other man, so that her husband would find her fresh and supple if he ever visited her from beyond the grave.

He got up from his bed, turned on the desk lamp in a single motion, and stared at the mosquito, thinking he could silence it if he only stared hard enough. Then he turned off the lamp to locate the mosquito but twenty seconds later turned it on again. For a moment he thought he would look at the pictures but instead found himself pacing in semicircles.

He was thinking of his visits to her room, of his whole relationship with her as a kind of humiliation. So many times he would leave her room on her terms—mystified, thwarted, beaten back by the image of her dead husband, a ghost. Why should she fill her days with so many favors for him but never offer him her body, if not to secretly humiliate him?

He stopped pacing and sat on the small brown circle of rug in the center of the room. He felt feverish and realized that he was soaked through with perspiration, his entire body so wet he imagined it must be glistening like the tips of her needles. He walked into the small bathroom and started drying himself with a towel. He was shaking slightly but persistently, and he felt dizzy.

He walked out of the bathroom and sat down on the bed, trying to think of what she was doing now, whether she could possibly be asleep or if instead she was listening for some trace of him, his smell or step. He could form a picture of her but he didn't know if she was calm or feverish, pacing or still. He merely saw the body underneath the filmy dress, a body that was made magnificent and then put into disuse. She might dye her hair, put on lipstick, cream her face, even lift her face, but her body was natural, it was part of his curse and it understood him (this infuriated him more than anything) better than the accumulation of all her sweet, supportive words.

He walked out into the hall now. Somehow he remembered to put on his slippers and to leave his door open an inch. All the corpses were asleep, even C. He could hear them gently wheezing. He was alone in the hallway, lit only by starlight from a small window just above the stairs. He was not sleepwalking yet he felt himself directed, walking assertively, though he was actually moving at a slow pace.

He would still leave in the morning but first he would visit her on his terms. It was not that he wanted or expected to seduce her;

rather, he would try to seduce her, or at least make her think he was seducing her, so that she would have to stop him. Stop him or let him, but at least admit by her decision what had happened the past year.

Her room was twice as large as his. Always it was heavy with the smell of her perfume, though the delicately flowered bedspread, the faded photographs on her bureau and desk, the old nineteenth-century-looking furniture had a different scent that coexisted with her body's insistently separate odor and always reminded him that she was indeed a much older woman.

She turned her head just before he knocked so that she was facing him in the dark when he entered. It was only then that he realized he must at first have some kind of cover story.

"It's Mason. Sorry to disturb you," he said softly, unconvincingly. "There was a terrible racket outside. I knew you'd heard it so I wanted to tell you that I went down with a flashlight to scout around and there's nothing to worry about."

"Thank you, Mason."

"Whatever was there came and went."

She said nothing and for several moments they were silent. He was standing only a few feet in front of the door, which was still open.

"I know how you worry," he said, already feeling himself lost.

"Thank you for being so brave in my defense."

He shifted his weight then regretted it immediately because the door creaked so loudly.

"So you're all right?"

"I believe I'm fine."

They were silent again. He saw her looking up at the ceiling at the same circle of space he had seen her stare at before. He thought she was trying to summon her husband, an image of him, not as he had been in the happiest, lightest days in the first year of their marriage, but a sterner image, more responsible, forbidding, profound. A composite image of father, husband, and her ultimate judge. The circle would save her again. She would locate her husband in it and he would save her because she knew why Mason had come and it was impossible.

Meanwhile he was shifting his weight and leaning toward the door. She wiped away the perspiration on her forehead with a handkerchief.

"I'll have the sweater finished for you soon. Then you can go out when it's cold at night without freezing."

"Thank you," he said.

"I'm sorry I aggravated you by talking about the partnership today. I just want what's best for you."

"I know. I'll think it over."

"Well, two new boarders will be here tomorrow," she said in a rush. "There's so much we'll have to do, don't you think so?"

He nodded, forgetting to say anything. He was thinking that he didn't hate her, that he was surprised that he didn't hate her after all this time.

"Good night, Mason. We'll have to get Floyd something for his throat, his coughing has been terrible lately."

He promised to pick up something when he went shopping and she thanked him. There was more silence. Now he only wanted to disappear, to have disappeared and never to have been there feeling like a child in this woman's room, who was old enough to be his mother, who was so old she was not even scared of him, who probably didn't even know why she did so many favors for him nor what the difference between kindness and humiliation was. (It occurred to him that this was what people meant by "love.")

They exchanged two more sentences he would never remember. It was like the inevitably bland talk on the radio. Somehow, unconsciously, he climbed the stairs. It was as if he were flying and walking at the same time.

Then, as soon as his door was shut, he went to his desk and picked up *Robinson Crusoe*. He took the pictures out without looking at them and walked into the bathroom, where he lit a match. A flame shot up—white, intense, burning through the sailboat in an instant, burning the water beneath it and turning to indistinguishable black Vicki's wide, relentless smile. When the flame got too high he doused it with water from the sink. For a minute he watched the dark crinkles of paper clinging to the sink's bottom and then shut off the light.

He was exhausted. The fire had been so beautiful that for a moment he thought of burning *Robinson Crusoe* too, but he decided not to. It was enough now to straighten his sheets and sleep. He was so tired he didn't even bother to turn the fan on, nor did he notice the mosquito still whining in the hot dead air above his bed.

Man without Memory

Although I once suffered from the same affliction, I haven't made it my business to meet many men without memories. Still, I've managed to familiarize myself with the small but growing literature about them. From what I've observed there are only two distinct types: amnesiacs who forget a particular part of their life, and those men for whom we have no medical term (perhaps because there are so few of them), who have no memories of any kind, even for a moment. These unfortunates, of whom I was once one, are simply unable to link any two moments together beyond performing the most rudimentary tasks. For instance, they remember to turn on a faucet to produce water but have no memory of ever drinking a particular glass of water. Each instant appears before them with a frightening autonomy. Instinctively they do certain things required to survive, but they have no sense of either their history or their future.

Need I add that men without memories are terribly vulnerable creatures, depending on everyone to be exactly who they say they are and to behave accordingly. In a word, they possess no data. It's not a case of their constantly forgetting, they simply can't retain recollections of any kind.

Maybe I should explain that, like amnesiacs, we men without memories often live normal lives in every respect before our illness. Unlike them, however, and frankly this makes our plight even more pitiful, there's rarely an accident or particular event to which we can trace our memory loss. Certainly this was the case with me. It's true that both my parents died within a year of each other, yet at least two years passed after that, years where I was moving from day to day with a reasonably adequate memory. What I'm insisting on is that there was no warning, that one awful, glittering morning I simply found myself nothing but the disconnected moment I was in.

Did I realize what had happened to me? I did have a vague sense of a dull, ongoing horror, but in those shapeless days I lived solely by reacting to phenomena. I "understood things," in other words, only after a situation was forced upon me. For example, my girlfriend, Andrea, might start a lovers' quarrel and I'd respond in the way I always did, although I had no memory of her that survived a single moment. Since I'm essentially the passive type, she apparently didn't detect enough variance in my behavior to ever question me seriously.

I stayed in my memoryless state (as I've later been able to reconstruct it) for about a month. But surely it's more interesting to describe how I recovered than to evoke a time when I was more like an educated animal than a human. It was steadfast, practical Andrea, though she was wholly ignorant of my condition, who literally led me to my cure. It was because she was in the habit of picking up after me, whether it be my floor, my person, or in this case my desk. One such time she found some papers she assumed were notes for an article I was writing. What she handed me instead was my only written record of my childhood, which I'd called "Lists and Principles of My Parents."

At first I stared at it, completely bewildered, understanding the denotative meaning of the words but unable to apply them to myself. I remember feeling something like a chill, and staring at the lists so long that Andrea finally grew alarmed.

That night two important things happened. When I looked at Andrea sleeping beside me I had a dim sense of who she was. This was so extraordinary that I constantly looked away and then back at her to reexperience it. Also, for the first time in many nights I thought of something that had happened to me the day before, mainly the feeling of the lists in my hand, the quiver they provoked in my flesh. I began to yearn for the morning so I could see the pages in the daylight. The remarkable progress here is that I remembered what a morning was and so could anticipate it.

With the first sign of sun I continued my staring therapy—first by my window, then on a hill behind the museum. I have no idea how long each session was, nor even how many days they lasted before the image of my father's face and then my mother's became clear to me on the pages, slowly, and in stages, the way a photograph develops.

In the same way that I slowly recognized my parents, actual scenes from my childhood that my lists alluded to became memories again. Here is the time to state emphatically that childhood diaries or records of any kind have no general medical application for men without memories. The grim reality is that there is no agreed-upon cure for us. Many of us simply don't recover, and for those who do, no two ever have been observed to do it the same way. What I report about my condition and the "Lists and Principles" that cured it may well have no practical bearing for anyone beyond myself, and I would be immodest and irresponsible to pretend otherwise.

But what were these "Lists and Principles"? At first they were merely observations about my parents begun just before my teenage years, all grouped under two different headings: "Things That Are Important to My Father," and then apparently to be fair about it, "Things That Are Important to My Mother." I'd list them numerically and whenever I deduced a general law I'd write in my principle. For example, I wrote "Father and Mother argue about the summer house at the kitchen table while I watch them from behind the door." From this came the principle of "One Watches Two," for as I was an only child, and moreover steered away from those friendships that usually populate one's childhood, I invariably watched them alone. This simple law of perception in itself proved invaluable as an aid to recovering my past, fixing in a single statement many of the impressions of my lists and giving me as well a whole series of associated memories.

At that stage my memory of my origins was approximately half recovered, but I was less successful in making sense of my present circumstances, though some progress was achieved there as well.

For instance, I'd advanced from doing purely by instinct those things essential to my survival to attaining a certain level of reflection. I now knew as soon as I was told that I was a director of the Museum of Modern Graphic Art, located near a college in western Massachusetts, and that I was, fortunately, on a half-year sabbatical. I also understood that Andrea had for some time been my "constant female companion"—for the concept of time was beginning to assume some importance to me. I now no longer performed coitus instinctively but realized it must have a significance of a kind, not only in my life, but for all people—whether they had memories or not. As for Andrea, a rather overeducated psychology student from a neighboring college, I understood that she must have special characteristics for me to do this with her and was convinced I would eventually recall them.

For several weeks I remained in this state until one afternoon when I was riding my bicycle around Andrea's campus. It happened that on this bicycle trip I spotted her professionally eccentric visiting lecturer from the philosophy department, conceived of by his students as brilliant, in reality a dolt, walking in his slippered feet across the football field. The sight of that bearded pretender trying to look as if he were meditating while he moved so lightly over the yardlines from lack of energy, not grace, somehow gave my mind its needed jolt. I promptly cycled back to my room to study my lists, first closing my blinds, locking my door, and disconnecting the phone, so Andrea wouldn't disturb me. Instantly I was flooded with a rich and vivid sense of my childhood, both in a general sense and in the dazzling particulars my lists described. When I returned to myself and looked around the room I felt exhilarated, humbled by the richness of every object around me. My eraser, for instance—I understood its mission for the first time. I felt its essential nobility as it destroyed countless ineffectual sentences I'd been writing throughout my life. It was the same with the venetian blinds, devoted as they were to protecting my privacy and sleep, and to my bedspread, which covered me each night as I went over my day's work or else lay calmly over me as I looked at my lists and remembered my parents.

All of this I attribute to the lists I wrote as a child and which I quote in part below, with the reminder that the actual lists that finally cured me were five times as long for my father, perhaps three times as long for my mother. I reserve the right of some privacy in these matters. After all, it's the law itself that's more important than its particulars. With this in mind I offer these examples directly from my lists:

Things That Are Important to My Father

1. Father likes to smoke a pipe, but only after putting on his darkest pair of sunglasses. It may be he believes his pipe won't work unless his sunglasses are on first and properly aligned.
2. Most of the time Father stays indoors. When he's inside he wears his dark blue slippers and walks so quietly on the rug (and almost our entire house is carpeted) that he scarcely makes a sound.
3. Father spends much of his time reading books. The last few weeks whenever I watched him his face was behind one.
4. My view of Father is never completely clear. When he's in his bedroom or study a door is partially closed or completely shut (in which case I have to look through a keyhole). When he occasionally goes outdoors and sits on the patio I'm afraid he'll see me, although I'm very thin, so I hide behind my bedroom curtains or else behind the porch door.

Principle: In the process of being formulated.

Are you surprised at how few examples there are, or that they are so utterly mundane? I assure you I'm clear about their limited objective value and unashamed to insist on their stature as supreme personal poetry. I merely ask you to remember that the lists gave me back my memory, or in effect kept me a man. It would be impossible for me not to revere them. Onward to Mama, then!

Things That Are Important to My Mother

1. Once in the bathroom, Mother often leaves the door half open. When she calls me to her room to tell me something, I see her breasts reflected in the bathroom mirror. No matter when I look at her, her eyes meet mine.

2. Around the house Mother wears full-length dresses, but to do her back exercises she wears a pink silk nightgown. The exercises are done on her floor at two different speeds: slow, as if she's lifting weights with her legs, and fast, as if she's riding a bicycle as quickly as she can. If I should ever not look down and see her on the floor, I'll find her kicking legs reflected in her bedroom mirror.
3. Mother cries almost as often as she talks. Sometimes when she makes me soup I wonder if she's put in some of her tears, which I'll somehow have to swallow.
4. Detesting loneliness, Mother keeps company with her white toy poodle. At times she hugs it so tightly the poodle cries. In the winter she covers every inch of the dog with little scarves and bright pink sweaters.

Yes, these excerpts are also poor in number, and poetry, and logic too, and yet they contain a world of time for me. Andrea, however, displayed an obvious antipathy toward my lists. Once, shortly after my memory returned, she surprised me with a visit and found me studying them. It happened that I'd forgotten, in a normal absent-minded way, that she expected me to attend some campus function with her. She stood defiantly in front of me by my desk, her strawberry blonde hair newly coiffeured, her face rouged, her lipstick stuck on too brightly, and for a moment I was depressed that I still remembered her. Before I could begin to dream up an apology she snatched the lists from my desk, and turning her back on me walked to the other side of the room.

"I want to see what's so important to you that you totally forgot about the evening you'd planned to spend with me."

I felt an equal mix of rage and terror for my lists were my only assurance that I would never lose my memory again, and unless you've suffered my loss you can never appreciate how much a man who was once without memory always fears his condition will return. Still, I was able to compose myself while Andrea continued her indictment.

"It's those same papers I always see you with! Christ, you wrote this when you were a child, didn't you? It's all about your father and mother whom you've never even bothered to tell me about no matter how often I've asked you."

Normally I would have stayed silent, for Andrea wasn't a person who was comfortable being angry. Instead, anger seemed to go in and out of her like a poison that once swallowed was immediately rejected. The wisest thing would be to let her tantrum run its course and then make my apology. Nevertheless, I answered automatically that I never thought she was interested in my past. Her eyes seemed to grow brighter and darker simultaneously. "Not interested? If I'm not interested in you who am I interested in? Why do I drive over here every day from my school to see you? Why do I sleep with you at night?"

She had several good points here. Still, it wasn't possible to tell her the simple truth, mainly, that when she asked me about my parents I didn't remember them any more than I remembered her. The truths of non-memory were just too awful and confusing for the uninitiated to benefit from, much less comprehend. I had to keep them hidden. Instead I tried another approach. I launched into a rare monologue, declaring my unequivocal passion, her goodness, my need for her. I convinced her that where she saw a conflict I saw two kindred spirits.

"So what do you do when you find a kindred spirit?" she asked, smiling.

"I don't know," I said innocently.

"I'll show you," she said, putting one arm around my neck and the other around my skinny rear.

I don't remember what happened next, but all men suffer a kind of amnesia when they try to describe sex. I do know that when it was over I began to feel guilty. I decided to make up for my missed date and immediately invited her to dinner, then topped that with an invitation to the theater. Andrea looked skeptical—it had probably been a long time since I'd invited her anywhere—but she was soon nodding her head, her hair making a delicious swishing sound.

In the days before my date with Andrea I concluded that my memory of my present was adequate but my lists were still dangerously incomplete. Although I had many more entries for my father than my mother, I still hadn't found a single principle for him. I began to concentrate exclusively on finding this absent material, hoping that by repeating staring sessions with my lists I might find the missing principle. I'd stare at them either in my room or in my favorite corner of the museum—first from a certain distance at the form of my penmanship itself, then up as close as I could.

Once, after performing these rituals, I saw an image of my parents walking together on a beach, my mother accompanied by the dog, my father impeccably dressed with his sunglasses fitting over his eyes, as she said to him, "Why do you have to always be so . . . mature? Why can't we . . ." (no notes on the rest of that though I strained to hear). Was I along with them or else hiding behind a sand dune or a palm tree? I couldn't be sure.

These were excruciating exercises and my only relief came from thinking of Andrea from time to time. Who knows, it might have helped me if I'd moved around a bit, but in those days I seemed rooted to one spot. I don't recall leaving my apartment except for brief trips to the supermarket. The truth is, I spoke to no one, nor did I feel any desire to bicycle. Occasionally I'd peek at the clouds, for I enjoyed checking their movements. Somehow I associated the sun with my mother, the lofty shifting clouds with my father. For Andrea, I found no analogue in nature, but she wasn't diminished any for that. In fact, I took special precautions to be sure I wouldn't forget our plans again. I even surrounded my rooms with an assortment of clocks, watches, and other timepieces, all set for her arrival at seven o'clock. I took a kind of pride in my new relationship with clocks, imbued with meaning as it now was. Before they were simply oddly shaped disks, decorated with completely incomprehensible designs. Now they told me when they were bringing me someone I remembered and wanted to see. I began to feel an unrestrained admiration for them, a genuine passion in the Spinozan sense of the word.

My efforts were rewarded! My strategy paid off! I was dressed, combed, cologned—a perfect match for my well-groomed guest. She, in turn, was flushing in triumph at my new punctuality as we drove off in her cozy sports car to the closest thing to an elegant

restaurant our town had to offer. At first all went smoothly, as we
drank sparkling wine and picked at our lobsters. Andrea was ebul-
lient; in fact, I'd never remembered her laughing so much. She kept
making remarks about my manliness and running her fingers
through my dark but otherwise undistinguished hair. It was as if she
were rewarding me for not devoting myself to my lists, which she all
but said kept me a child.

I put up with these thinly veiled insults happily enough, for I was
in far too good a mood to be hurt, and besides, her smell, her
breasts, her eyes were more alluring than ever. It was only after she
excused herself to go to the ladies' room that I felt the lists for some
reason sticking out of the back pocket of my pants. I was both
shocked that I'd been so careless to take them with me and afraid
that I'd lose them, for I had no copies. The reader should know I
never considered that my lists could have copies—their form and
color were not possible to reproduce on a machine. Indeed, those
surface qualities were as important to me as the actual content.
Consequently, I had to sit with one hand on my pocket throughout
the remainder of dinner, as well as through a soporific five-act
melodrama. As if this weren't difficult enough, pictures of Mother
taking her poodle on yet another grand tour of my childhood home,
or of Father pacing the study in his slippered feet, his inevitable pipe
stuck in his mouth, kept appearing before me. It was impossible not
to transmit some of this to Andrea, I felt, and yet she was still
smiling as we drove back from the play—her hand on my thigh
while mine stayed firmly planted on my lists.

In my apartment she grew immediately affectionate. "Darling,"
she said, smiling radiantly, "we're having fun like we used to. Do
you remember our trip to Boston. It was so beautiful, so exciting,
and you know what? I'm just as excited again, even more." She
grasped my hand, I assumed to undo my pants. It was only when she
met with my instinctive resistance that she bound up from beneath
me and demanded to see what I was hiding. What could I do? I had
to show her.

"Oh my God," she screamed, "it's those baby papers again! I
don't believe this." She gathered up her clothes even more quickly
than she'd removed them. "Look," she said, shaking an admon-
ishing finger at me, "get rid of that baby stuff or get rid of me.

Make up your mind, Mr. Curator.'' And in a few stunning instants
she was fully dressed and had slammed the door behind her. As
always, once she moved it was with incredible speed.

Did I follow her or ask her to stop and reconsider? I didn't, yet a
curious thing happened. Before that evening, whenever I had an
unpleasant experience I'd will it away. This was an especially easy
technique to develop—whenever I looked at my lists for even the
memory of my father silently serving himself from a bowl of soup
or of my mother blinking wildly as she drove the family car, Father
sitting straight as a corpse beside her, could hold me for hours and
provide a complete escape from my circumstances. Now this strictly
diversionary value of my lists no longer worked, and my pain stayed
within me.

Andrea had left in a huff. When she felt really slighted her temper
could be ferocious and could last considerably longer than when she
was merely ''angry.'' Once, before my memory had fully returned,
I'd stared at a waitress to see if I knew her. At that time I was still
wondering if I'd once known many people I was actually seeing for
the first time. Something in the way the waitress watched me made
me wonder, but it turned out I was mistaken. To impulsive Andrea,
of course, there was no explaining it. Then, as now, she simply got
up and walked off with no hint of when she'd return.

I was sure of one thing—when she was upset it was still best to
leave her alone. So I resolved to forget about her for a while and
instead returned to my lists with renewed vigor, studying in particular the entries from one of my childhood summers in Tanglewood.

Father and Mother attend the Sunday night concerts regularly.
Mother brings her handkerchief and cries during the symphony.
Father sits behind his sunglasses and leans forward when there is
silence between the movements.

The truth is this entry, and the memories surrounding it, was the
only one strong enough to ward off those images of Andrea that were
now raiding my mind persistently. For some reason, in that setting
of decaying nature and pseudoculture, my parents, though they
weren't happier, were maybe trying harder to be, which made this
entry especially precious. Staring at it I'd remember returning from

my usual swim after the concert and then pausing at the end of the path to our summer house to watch my father. Once I saw him standing five feet in front of a birch tree in the backyard, his arms raised like a mechanical soldier. He looked to be surveying the tree, but I couldn't be sure. Above the tiger lilies in front of our canoe, three dragonflies hovered. The sun hung tentatively while I studied the scene and found myself feeling like the birch tree.

That night at dinner Mother said, "Why shouldn't I eat my sundae, I have little enough sensual pleasure in my life." Then the dog cried and Mother changed its scarf. Meanwhile Father sat at the kitchen table studying his stocks, sipping his tea spoonful by spoonful. Why did I always think he was somehow communing with his teaspoon, as if he were confiding his secret life to it? I had no answer, probably because I had no principle for him and was still no closer to finding one than I was to locating new memories of my mother.

It seemed my search for my tearful, voluptuous mother and my dignified but remote father would be a long one, perhaps endless, and my spirit all but sank. Is it any wonder, then, that when Andrea called me a few days later and demanded a meeting at my apartment I accepted without thinking of her motivations?

She arrived in a no-nonsense business suit, with sunglasses of her own that she quickly removed. We were facing each other a few feet apart—she on the bed, I at my desk chair. She wasted no time in getting to the point.

"You know I've had the most incredible fantasies about you, but I was all wrong." Her hands moved from her knees to just under her breasts, as if to emphasize their fullness. "I used to be convinced it was another woman, but now I see how preposterous that was. It's nothing more than that damn diary, that's what you're obsessed with. I think you secretly want to stay a child and you think that little fetish will help you."

Once again, she'd scarcely been with me five minutes and she already had me shaking.

"It isn't true. I never meant to hurt you."

I could see by her sullen expression that I needed to say much more than this.

"Why is it that you always tell me what you never meant to do and never what you do mean to do?"

"I don't follow."

"You don't follow. For God's sake you're a brilliant man. You run a small but first-rate museum. You've published articles in some top-notch art journals. You have a real future in your field. How can you not know what you want? Do you know if you want me?"

"Of course I do."

"Why don't you tell me about your diary? Why is it so important to you?"

"It isn't so important."

"Why are you lying again? You spend practically all your time with it. You sometimes even bring it to bed with us, and if it's not actually in your pants like the last time, it's on your mind. Can't you see it divides us, that it keeps you from living?"

"I just sometimes miss my parents. I never expected them to die so young, and my diary, as you call it, helps me remember them. Is that so shameful? It's nothing I can't overcome," I said, forcing a smile. More was needed, for she still wasn't budging.

"Andrea, I need you. I'm lost without you. Give me one more chance, that's all. Come here," I said, extending my arms. She looked at me as if considering something, then said "I'm the one on the bed," coolly brushing aside a lock of hair and smiling.

Once more her anger left her, and with few more words being said we embraced. Shortly after we made love she fell asleep. When I looked at her she seemed to be smiling as if inviting me to join her. It was an invitation I never considered. To begin with, once I became a man without memory sleep was rarely an easy proposition. When I had no memory, every moment was actually like being asleep and then constantly being awakened. Moreover, after my memory returned I always feared I'd lose it again while I was sleeping. Each time I woke up I'd immediately run to my lists and give myself a memory check. Remembering this, I looked at my clock that glowed in the dark and watched five full minutes go by, then another five. I felt chilled and began to pull up my blankets. Suddenly I stopped short. I was thinking of the lists again, worrying that somehow in the dark the magic formula of words would come undone and get hopelessly tangled. Now that I had a chance to study them it was foolish to wait.

In a moment I slid out from under the covers and tiptoed to my desk. The words were still in their proper places, I could see that in a glance, but I'd scarcely begun to study them when I knew I was being watched. I looked up and found myself staring at Andrea's unblinking eyes.

Incredibly, she'd woken up and caught me with my lists! Of course I tried to hide them as fast as I could, but all the time she was watching me. Not knowing what else to do, I got up from the desk and walked mechanically back to bed, hoping she might somehow think I was sleepwalking.

No arms were there to greet me. Instead, she turned her back to me and pulled the covers up to her neck. I lay on top of the blankets without any kind of plan. I thought of caressing her back but instead stayed still. Then I decided to adopt my standard approach and wait for her anger to subside, imagining that in the morning the incident might be forgotten. But I grew increasingly uneasy. Far off I could hear a car coming, then the doors shut. Some lovers returning home, I thought, much happier than I was. My happiness had its back turned toward me, and I could merely lie in the dark watching it.

When your memory returns your dreams return with it, and with something to dream about you're able to sleep. How else can I explain that with every intention of waiting for Andrea to turn toward me I fell asleep, and that when I woke up she'd vanished. At first I was simply too astonished to feel anger, but that came soon enough, coupled with the fear that as a final act of vengeance she'd destroyed my lists or taken them with her. That got me out of bed in a hurry. On top of my desk, where I hoped to find my lists, I discovered these terse lines:

I have found the strength to do the inevitable—I have left you and will not contact you again. I don't think you're a mean man, just a very ill one. If you can't find a way to extricate yourself from your childhood fetish and all it means to you, I hope you'll seek some professional help. Don't look for me.—Andrea

I let her note drop from my hands and started to look for my lists, which had left my desk as suddenly as her note had appeared. Was this the horrible revenge she'd conceived for me, maybe in that unblinking moment when we stared at each other a few hours ago in the dark? Could she have been stupid enough or self-important enough to have stolen them—stolen my very memories—in an effort "to help me"? Were there no limits to her arrogance? Now that her studies were advancing in psychology, had she confused herself with the "professional help" she thought I needed and unilaterally made a decision to tamper with my private property "for my benefit"?

I tried to figure out how I could prove what she'd taken. In my frenzied state I imagined whole scenarios where I confided in sympathetic detectives, then how they would cross-examine her and retrieve my lists. When these fantasies dissolved I was forced to face the possibility that I would once again become a man without memory. This was something I was unprepared for mentally or physically. This was too strong a revenge for anyone to take. It was true I'd unwittingly wasted Andrea's love, but to steal my lists would be going too far. Although I hadn't told her their secret, she must have sensed what they meant to me even as she cursed them.

In a single moment my room turned bright orange. I felt rudderless, dizzy. I blinked repeatedly and covered my eyes for fear I'd be blinded, but the light grew brighter and still more punishing. Before I could move for shelter the objects in the room started to unravel from their fixtures as if they were erupting. The blinds shook, the clocks started circulating around my head, my bed began thumping with increasing speed. I screamed once, twice, and then scattered the papers on my desk like a wild man.

In the course of my attack I knocked over a monograph on M. C. Escher and saw my lists underneath them. I regained my breath and in an instant the orange light disappeared, the blinds ceased rattling, the clocks settled, the bed stayed still.

I didn't pause to contemplate this miracle; neither did I weep or thank any heavenly powers for my lists. I simply held my lists more firmly than ever and read them through again as quickly and thoroughly as I could. Never did I hold them with more gratitude, or read them with more concentration, yet nothing had changed. None of my memories were missing, but neither had I gained any new ones of my mother, nor had I any leads for my father's principles.

I was exhausted. I checked through the papers once more and then, after locking them away in my desk, walked to the museum. I decided to spend the day preparing as best I could to go back to work. We had a new exhibition of South American prints scheduled in a week—my sabbatical was over. Preparing for work was a routine matter, and after the events of the morning it was so routine it scarcely held my attention.

In the middle of the afternoon, when my mind once again wandered, I began to visualize Andrea's hair. I tried several times to write her a letter but eventually abandoned it for I couldn't find the proper tone. It was pointless to write her anyway since what I really wanted was a letter *from* her. The sad fact was that the only letter I had from her was her goodbye note. Though her college was nearby it would be very difficult to see her if she wanted to avoid me and impossible to make her acknowledge me, for I sensed her resolve to forget me. No more softening stares or open arms. It was awful to contemplate. I certainly couldn't spend any more time thinking about it in my office or I'd start screaming. . . .

It grew dark over my hideous museum. I returned to my apartment and cooked dinner in my melancholy kitchenette. It wasn't long before I began worrying that I might have lost my lists again, that while I was away they might have wandered off and left me. So it was that I went to my desk and unlocked it and spent several hours with them. I read over and over about the spoonfuls of tea, the crying poodle, the kicking legs reflected in the mirror, the dark sunglasses and somber pipe. In my mind's eye I watched my father's slippered walk, saw my mother vengefully eating ice cream, saw them sitting rigidly, expectantly, at an anonymous concert. And while I contemplated the rich but inadequate treasures of my memory I also saw Andrea's glistening eyes and open arms. It was curious, but along with my feverish quest for my past I felt an unmistakable longing for the present.

Aerialist

First I want to write what my impressions were of the apartment and what my life was like before the change. I'd intended to take an apartment on the second floor (due to my fear of heights), but after I paid my deposit the manager told me the only place still available was a large studio on the top floor, the thirty-third. I was told I'd be living at the highest point in the city.

When I saw it for the first time the sun came through the windows lighting up the just-shampooed carpet. It was so extraordinary I forgot about my fear right away and spent four hours feverishly unpacking. I thought, My whole life is here, all my possessions, but there are so many closets they'll all be tucked out of view. Besides wall-to-wall carpeting the apartment came with a brand-new stove and refrigerator, a laundry room two doors away, an exercise room in the basement, a dry cleaners on the main floor where there was also a maildrop, and newspapers on sale in the lobby. It's all a very good marketing strategy, I remember thinking. They want to get you dependent on the building so they put everything in it.

But the most remarkable thing about the apartment was the view. Eight large plate-glass windows covered the length of the studio. There was so much space and so many things to see it was a completely new puzzle every day. Looking left to right I could see the museum, the railroad tracks, center city itself—with high-rises, banks, office buildings, and an elementary school playground where children were always playing basketball. Farther to the right were Veterans' Stadium, the Walt Whitman Bridge, some trees, and a slice of the river. In the mornings everything was bright and at night there were lights everywhere—search lights, streetlights, office lights, lights reflected in glass.

In many ways the apartment was the opposite of where I'd lived before on Pine Street. I'd spent a year in an area filled with prostitutes, in a third-floor walk-up with low ceilings and uncarpeted floors. My windows looked directly into the apartment of a woman in the adjoining building who had never bothered to buy a window shade for her room. Every time I'd get back from the bank I'd sense she was looking at me, whether she actually was or not. It was pull down the shades and live like a bat or feel her eyes on me, and when you're a teller peoples' eyes are on you all day long. As it turned out, however, I began to watch her. Her name was Lisa and her occupations, I quickly learned, were modeling and studying art.

I soon found myself following a routine. I'd come back from work, turn on the TV, and watch Lisa during the commercials. When it was time to eat I'd bring my TV dinner into the room. Shortly after the eleven o'clock news she'd shut off her lights and I'd usually go out for a walk, down Spruce or Locust and then circle back to my place. One night I saw a banner draped across Locust Street:

An Evening of Cha Cha
A Benefit for AIDS

It occurred to me that there was a lot of dying in my neighborhood, which happened in all neighborhoods, of course, but this was contagious dying. Halfway down the block a group of prostitutes were running and laughing whenever they saw a police car, as if they were trying to outrun a wave at the beach. Meanwhile, on the corner, a boy was pretending to use a pay phone so he'd look like he had a reason to be on the street. He was, of course, hoping to be picked up. A bottle crashed behind me and a drunk started screaming at the sky. I figured that's enough for tonight and I went back to Pine Street.

When I walked into my room I saw Lisa lying in her bed reading *Jokes and Their Relation to the Unconscious*. Just before I pulled the shade she looked up at me from Freud and our eyes met. I turned off the lights and tried to get to sleep but I kept seeing images of her face, which was pretty and round and lit by bright, light eyes. Once I watched her talking and laughing with a man who had just finished working on her portrait, and I noticed a slight and very appealing space between her teeth. The man was probably a fellow student, or maybe a young teacher or a young-looking teacher. He was one of her most frequent visitors and once accompanied her to a modeling agency while I followed less than a block behind. I began to suspect that he might be in her room now and debated whether I should pull up my shade. Eventually I compromised by walking to the side of the window and moving the shade a few inches.

My suspicions were correct. They were in her room, lit only by a dull gold lamp on the floor. She was wearing the nightshirt she normally slept in and he had on a shiny pair of pink satin pants. At first I thought they might be rehearsing some kind of play, their gestures were so sweeping and theatrical, until I realized they were actually making love. That surprised me. I knew Lisa to be earnest, idealistic, accommodating, even a little passive, but in the scene I watched she was both the aggressive star and the director.

I felt hurt and disappointed. I'd always found something depressing about combining theater with sex, something I may even have considered evil, yet I watched, as I'd watched every other aspect of her life in her room. In a little while I wondered if she might not be performing for me. After all, I was her devoted audience, our eyes had met many times and many times I'd thought of signaling to her and saying out my window, "Look, we've watched each other for a year, why don't we say hello?" I'd also considered calling her and asking her out, of course, but didn't. There were the usual inhibiting factors, not the least of which was my dark and disgusting apartment.

That night I forced myself to confront certain truths about Lisa. I'd watched her so much, and occasionally followed her, because I was attracted to her. From my eyes alone I'd, in a way, fallen in love with her. I'd pursued no other women because I wanted Lisa, but what, really, could I offer her? As long as I lived in this cave I'd never be able to call her, and as long as I stayed where I was I'd continue to watch her and that obviously wasn't a healthy situation for me.

At the bank the next day I applied for a special loan available to five-year employees. One of the tellers named Frank told me about the high-rise and how my social life would improve if I moved there. He said I owed it to myself to live better. A month later (exactly six weeks ago), I moved in.

I know now that the change began then, though I didn't realize it at the time. That it happened to me validates my idea of God as being unconcerned with human notions of status. For who could have been more ordinary than I was? I'd worked at three or four jobs since I graduated from college. I'd never been married, though I had one "wife equivalent" back in the '70s in a different city. Always I'd lived in a marginally middle-class way. If there was anything unusual about me, besides being an underachiever, it was my lack of a social life. Before the change I had no real friends at the bank, no girlfriend, no one I was even fantasizing about except Lisa. My father was an accountant, my mother a substitute English teacher. I saw them three times a year in Poughkeepsie. And then the change.

The first time I felt some inkling of it was when I started to look out my new windows for long periods of time. Apparently my apartment was in the middle of so many competing signals that none of the TV channels came in well and with most of them I saw double. So I started to stare at my view. One morning I got up earlier than usual. When I raised my shades I was shocked. Great patches of color were in the sky forming a huge belly of purple with a salmon orange underbelly. Submerged beneath that was a stream of light green. As the orange intensified it suffused the purple, making it look like an enormous crater. Meanwhile, when I looked again at the green part, I saw that it wasn't really "green" at all but that there was no other word for it. A flock of birds appeared, forming a kind of figure eight in front of the crater. Then the sun split the crater like a bomb slowly exploding upward and my apartment was filled with warm orange light. I couldn't take my eyes off all of this and was ten minutes late for work.

I went to bed early that night to be sure I'd wake up in time for tomorrow's sunrise. (Needless to say I'd stopped pulling my shades down at night.) In a few days I discovered that there was always drama in the sky equal to that first sunrise, always more colors and shapes than there were words for, and always more order than I could conceive.

Why did it take me so long to understand, I wondered? Why hadn't I seen this before? I tried to recall other times I might have looked at the sky and could only remember watching a fly ball in a baseball park or some construction workers on top of an office building or once, as a little kid in New York, ducking from a water-bomb someone threw at me from a high-rise. I hadn't noticed simply because I'd never watched.

After I began sky watching I quickly established a pattern of three hours of watching in the morning, then home during my lunch break for forty-five minutes, then two more hours in the late afternoon. Of course it was an inexhaustible subject, yet I felt I was learning things in a cumulative way. For instance, just from altering my position by a step in the living room I could make the moon appear, or when I lay down in bed with one pillow under my head instead of two I could make the skyline vanish and just see sky.

Once during my lunch break, while I was watching some clouds, I got so involved I forgot to go back to the bank. When this happened a second time Frank called to tell me that I'd better watch it, that the supervisor was getting angry and I was skating on thin ice. "You already can't afford your fancy apartment, what are you gonna do when you lose your job?" he said in a clipped, prissy tone.

I was tempted to tell Frank what was happening, but wisely I didn't. His whole world was Equi-bank. How could Frank at the bank understand? The sky was completely enveloping—everything was in it. It was also communicating to me, telling me things I needed to know and changing me in ways I couldn't express.

After my mother called to bawl me out for not calling on her birthday, I also didn't explain. The truth was that except for some images of Lisa, whom I sometimes saw after I finally closed my eyes and tried to sleep, the sky was all I thought about. I knew that the change was happening but I still struggled to keep a strong foothold in my everyday world. So I apologized to my mother and sent her flowers, and I began setting my alarm clock to ring forty-five minutes after I'd come back to my apartment during lunch break, which helped my attendance at the bank.

By then I'd bought two six-by-four mirrors and put one on the living room table in front of the through-space to the kitchen and the other against the wall where the television used to be. (I'd long ago put my TV away in the storage closet.) Now, in those rare moments when I accidentally wasn't facing the windows, I had a way of monitoring the sky. I was living in a state of constant expectation, but I was constantly having my expectations fulfilled. Really, I was simply experiencing the natural rhythms of the change, so of course there was no way my watches could ever disappoint me.

But how did I manage to go to the bank every day and concentrate on my job? It's true I'd sometimes see little suns where George Washington was supposed to be on the dollar bills, but somehow I got through that time with no major errors. Also, as my mental and spiritual strength increased I trusted my instincts more and they told me to keep going out into the world and to keep my job but to separate it completely from the time in my apartment. Toward that end I unplugged my phone a few weeks ago.

One morning right after I got up I was stopped by an image in the mirror. I turned around and found myself feeling each stage of the sun's rise into the heavens. I understood how we were related—how we were equals, really—both shot through with rays of divinity. I knew then that all entities are a part of God and that my purpose was to put this knowledge to active use. Immediately I decided to call Lisa.

This was the kind of decision that might have paralyzed me before, but now I merely had to think of a single sunray for a second to feel sure of myself and begin dialing. I told her I'd been her neighbor and had often wanted to speak with her; that I'd definitely planned to call her when a stroke of good fortune happened and I'd moved. I gave her my new address and she seemed impressed. Then I asked if I could see her, but she hesitated. There was actually an embarrassing silence during which I asked if she remembered me. "Maybe," she said and hung up.

I refused to be discouraged. Instead I went straight to my windows and had a meditation with a pale white cloud. When it was over I knew my next move. I remembered that I'd followed her on three separate Wednesdays to the Star Watch Modeling Agency and that the agency closed at five. The next day I was waiting in front of the agency with a bouquet of roses.

Lisa was so heavily made up I almost didn't recognize her. She was wearing skin-tight pants, and for a moment I wondered what kind of modeling she did, before realizing that it no longer mattered.

"Hi, I'm your old neighbor who phoned you the other day. I brought these for you," I said, holding the roses out to her. She looked uncertain whether to accept them but her hands finally took them as if they'd made the decision independently from her.

"So what's this all about?" she asked, looking at me skeptically but half smiling.

"I just want to talk to you for a few minutes. Can I walk with you for a while?"

"I'm catching a bus on Chestnut," she mumbled, increasing her speed.

"May I walk you to your stop?"

"I guess. So what are you, the last chivalrous man in the city or something?"

"I hope you like roses."

"Who doesn't like roses? They're really pretty."

"Actually they're a bribe because I need to speak to you and I need to show you something very important."

"Oh, yeah?"

"Yes. Right now as a matter of fact."

"Is this the part where you rip open your raincoat?"

"No, it's nothing like that," I said, feeling wounded but laughing along with her. I was glad she had a sense of humor. It wasn't an entirely appropriate thing to say but I had to remember that I'd changed and she hadn't. I decided to go slowly and stick to small talk for the rest of our walk.

"Well, what can I say?" she said, indicating the flowers. "You've made my day. Look, here's my bus, thanks again for the roses."

I smiled and waved goodbye, perhaps once too often, but I did manage to keep her smiling.

For the next three days I wired her different kinds of flowers, which gave me the excuse to call her each day to ask how she liked them. On the first day she said, "You're really something. I love orchids, they look nice with the roses." On the second day I sent daisies and her enthusiasm diminished a little.

"My apartment's starting to look like a hothouse. By the way, I hope you're rich, otherwise I'm gonna start to feel bad about this."

"Forget about the money. I just want to see you soon. I have to tell you something extremely important."

"Tell me now. You obviously know how to get my attention."

"It would be better in person."

She paused. "We'll see," was all she said.

On the third day I sent lilies and called her a little later than I normally did.

"Look, it's been a lot of fun and I'm very flattered but please stop."

"Why? I thought you liked them."

"I loved them all but it's starting to get creepy, getting them every day from someone I don't really know."

"But I would love to get to know you."

"Well let's start by stopping the flowers, okay? It's making me nervous."

"I'm sorry."

"It's just that my intuition, not to mention my experience, says that with gifts come expectations. You know what I mean?"

"I only mean to give you an infinitely greater gift."

"I'll bet," she said, laughing.

"No, you don't understand. . . . Look, I promise I'll stop if you'll just meet me for coffee someplace, okay?"

She hesitated but finally agreed to meet me two days later. Of course I kept my part of the bargain and stopped sending her flowers. I unplugged my phone again and spent my time at home watching the sun rise and feeling the change and at night feeling my closeness with the stars. I also began reading, really for the first time since college, because I was curious to find out about other people's experience of change. I read parts of Dante's *Divine Comedy* and *St. Augustine's Confessions* and all of Franz Kafka's "Metamorphosis.'' The Kafka story was very interesting. Of course his character's metamorphosis was backward and mine was completely forward, but I could still relate to it, as they say.

When I wasn't sky watching or reading I'd think about Lisa. What a busy, contradictory soul she had! She was so sweet and funny, but I also had to remember (as if I could ever forget) that she was the same person who wore those skin-tight clothes on the street, who didn't even bother to buy a shade for her room, and who stood over her painter friend that way. Clearly, she was a soul in peril who needed to channel her energy into a higher form. Did she ever look at the sky and see what was there? It was up to me to show her and the rest what would happen naturally, as it had for me, I was sure of it. After all, isn't the world proof that good people can sometimes do evil things?

. . . In the coffee shop I was both polite and restrained and only flattered her selectively. Toward the end I finally told her that I had a secret that had changed my life.

"So am I supposed to guess it?" she said, smiling just wide enough for me to see the little space between her teeth.

"You're suppose to *see* it."

"Are you a mystic or one of those 'New Age' people or something?"

I shook my head. "It can change your life too. You just have to come to my apartment for ten minutes and I'll show you."

"I'll bet. Wow, what an original approach you have."

"It's not an approach. Why are you so skeptical?"

"You think so? I was just wondering why I keep listening to you."

"Because you sense that I'm honest, you can feel me telling you the truth."

She still wouldn't agree to anything definite, but I sensed she was weakening.

The next day when I called she said she'd come over at five o'clock for fifteen minutes. I hung up and began dancing all over my carpet. But after I finished dancing I realized there were many things to do. I had to vacuum the carpet, clean my living room table—which also functioned as a desk and dining table, clean the kitchen and bathroom, and buy a bottle of gin, some cheese, and some fancy crackers. Later, while I was ironing my suit pants I remembered that toward the end of our meeting in the coffee shop she'd talked a lot about her career, to the point where I agreed that my secret would help that too. But would it? I only had to think about my miserable attendance record at the bank, the thin ice Frank said I was skating on, to feel anxiety about my own career. What was it that Lisa hoped for? I knew a lot about her in one sense, but she had many secrets that the darkness of her apartment made it impossible to know. Maybe this is a terrible mistake, I thought, turning away from the windows. But when I turned back I saw an image of myself smiling in the sun and I regained my confidence in an instant. Good thing, too, because my doorbell was ringing.

"Come right in," I said, cheerfully, extending my hand, which she shook. She was wearing a white dress with little pink flowers and pink lipstick that highlighted her full lips and made the little space between her teeth that much more exciting.

"You surprised I came?"

"You said you would, so of course I hoped you would."

"I decided to trust you," she said, still smiling a bit skeptically, I thought.

"Good decision," I said. The sun was pouring through me and I was speaking confidently and spontaneously, although this was my first date in half a year.

"Come in and sit down at the living room table."

"I can only stay a little while."

I decided not to respond to that. Instead I fixed two drinks in the kitchen. "Like one?" I said, after I returned from the kitchen. She nodded, skeptically of course.

"I'll sip it."

I sat down, half facing her, half facing the holy late afternoon light.

"I like your mirrors, they're really big."

"I don't want to miss a thing."

She looked down at her drink, blushing, and I said, "I mean with the sky. Incredible things happen every moment out there."

"It's a real impressive view."

I got up from my seat, drink in hand, and walked to the windows. "Everything is out there," I said, looking at the first signs of sunset reflected off an office building, then looking at her. "Why don't you come over here and look up? You can see better."

"I can see fine from here," she said, reaching for a cigarette and lighting it. "Why don't you tell me your news now. You said you had this important thing to tell me, remember."

"This is my news, this is my important thing," I said, indicating the sweep of the sky with my arms and spilling a couple of drops of gin on the carpet.

"I don't follow," she said, inhaling more rapidly on her cigarette.

"This is the power that's changed me. It's been in front of us all the time."

"You're talking about the sky or what?"

"Yes."

"How did it change you?"

"It tells me everything. It told me that my body may die but that I'm part of the world forever. It told me that I'm as much a part of God as anything or anyone. And it told me to call you."

She snuffed out her cigarette and looked down at the table. I saw her cheeks turn dark red.

"You're serious, aren't you?"

"Very much so."

"That's why you sent me the flowers and everything, so I'd see this?"

"I knew you couldn't see it where you lived, and I wanted you to be changed too. It's changing you even now. . . ."

"The sun is?"

"Yes, the sun, the sky, all of it. It's changing you even though you don't realize it. But if you spent a month or so watching it, you'd feel it in a totally overwhelming way."

"Well, it's certainly a beautiful view and thanks for sharing, but I think I'll be leaving now."

She got up from the table and walked toward the closet where her coat was.

"Wait. Please give me a minute more of your time. Two months ago, if someone said to me what I just did, I would've reacted the same way. Let me just explain why I asked you here instead of meeting you in some restaurant.''

"You already explained.''

"Just give me another minute.''

She looked surprised, or maybe frightened, but I went on.

"Have you ever noticed how our ideas of spirituality are connected with heights? How we say 'Our Father who art in Heaven'.''

"So this is supposed to be Heaven?''

"It's become Heaven.''

"And that would make you God?''

I smiled. "No more than you are.''

"Yeah, well the difference is I don't think I'm God so I don't try to play God with people's lives. See, I'm just a working girl plugging away at my humble career. I'm not really the religious type.''

"It can help more than your career. It can help you in every way.''

"What, looking out the window? Well, start a church then, charge admission. Call it the First Church of the High-Rise. Anyway, I'm going now.'' She opened the closet and pulled her coat off the hanger, which fell to the floor like a cymbal crashing. I rushed to the door and touched her arm.

"Hey, don't touch me, okay?''

"I'm sorry. Listen, everything I told you is true. I used to see you a lot when I lived next door to you and I thought you needed this.''

"Yeah, I remember you,'' she said just before she opened the door. "You used to try to watch me every time I got undressed. You didn't seem like God then and you don't now. Maybe you made some money, but it's just you in a high-rise.''

"You're trying to make me doubt everything.''

"No, really, I'm busy. I gotta go. Good luck with the sky,'' she said, closing the door. I pressed myself to the door and stared out the peephole and saw her running down the hallway toward the stairs. Ah, she wasn't even going to take the elevator, she was so eager to escape from me.

. . . After I watched Lisa leave I felt dizzy and sat down at the living room table. I closed my eyes and concentrated until all I saw in my mind's eye was a blank, clear area like a lineless piece of paper. When I was still in school and had to write in class I'd sometimes close my eyes and actually see the question I had to answer better. That was how I saw what I was thinking about now, like a question written on an empty piece of paper: "Is Lisa evil?" If she was simply confused and panicked in her confusion, if I maybe revealed too much too quickly, I could still call or write to her explaining things in a less-threatening way and everything could be saved. But if she planned to make me doubt myself the way I did when we were neighbors, that would call for a very different response.

. . . My head hurts. I find this excruciating to think about. I close my eyes again and feel like I'm on a roller coaster tilting downward, then like I'm a mere waterbomb dropping from a high-rise that space itself has cast down. Totally excruciating. I open my eyes and feel an urgent need for . . . . perspective.

I walk to the windows trying to keep my eyes above the building tops. The sun is setting on the other side of the high-rise, but I can see part of it reflected in the bank windows on 19th Street. I try to peer around my building to see the sunset better, but I can't. Meanwhile a cluster of birds fly by in different directions, although there are only supposed to be four major directions. Then I see an image of Lisa's face smiling in her dark apartment. I breathe deeply. I shudder. I hold onto the air conditioner and try to focus on my next move.

Carlin's Trio

1

It was the worst handshake of my life. It wasn't just the long up-and-down-overly-earnest shake itself, it was the way he made me feel that every part of him went into it. Then he did something that stunned me. He kept my hand in his about ten seconds longer than he should have, squeezing it and actually patting it with his other hand. All the while his wife was smiling at me like I was a blessed woman. As an afterthought he introduced her to me as Linda. A minute later Linda excused herself and trotted off to look at the swimming pool, then at the garden in back, getting down on her knees to examine the flowers as if they were pearls.

Immediately he started asking me questions. Did I like the Berkshires, did I come here often, what was I writing?

"Music," I said. I couldn't lie, because my notebook of composition paper was open on the table in front of my wicker chair on the porch. His face contorted like a hand puppet's. When it solidified it was trying to act impressed with me while also letting me know that he was just doing this because he was so nice.

"Are you a professional musician?" I felt my heartbeat quicken from anger.

"No, just an amateur."

"An amateur composer," he said (and I felt he was about to add, "that's really something for a girl to do"). "You must find Tanglewood inspirational."

I shrugged. "I just like getting away to the country. I've been coming here the last five summers."

"Where are you getting away from?"

"Pardon?"

"You didn't say where you lived when you weren't on vacation but I think I can tell. Is it Boston?"

"Cambridge, actually," and I smiled for a second.

"Are you a student there?" he said. The question, I realized later, was supposed to flatter me since I was twenty-eight years old and looked it.

"I have a business there."

The impressed-because-I'm-so-nice expression covered his face again. Naturally he asked me what kind of business and I told him I was part owner of a store that sells greeting cards and he acted like I'd discovered the cure for AIDS. Then I had to ask him a question, of course, and he told me he and his wife were from New York (Westchester), had never been to the Berkshires, that this inn (The Terrace) had been recommended to them, and that if I'd be kind enough he'd appreciate any suggestions I might have since I knew the area so well.

"Well, I'd better let you get back to your symphony," he said.

I was working on a piano trio. I thought he was going to find some way to touch me again, but he just gave me one of his astronaut smiles and went toward the garden to join Linda, who was patting the landlady's dog and making little baby sounds of pleasure. This was how I met Ralph and Linda Gilbert in the middle of July.

2

For three mornings in a row, I saw her sunning herself below my window. Her body was so beautiful it nearly made me gasp. She'd lie on a chaise lounge in the backyard, maybe forty feet away. The first two times she wore a light pink two-piece suit, risque but still something someone with a very good figure could wear in public. But on the third morning she outdid herself and switched to an off-white suit, almost indistinguishable from her skin. She always repeated the same ritual, wearing a white beach jacket which she'd immediately put on the back of the chaise lounge. In her hands she'd carry a James Bond novel and a half-used tube of suntan lotion which she applied slowly, stretching her body in all directions as she did it. After she finished spreading the lotion over her legs and thighs (she spread it over her thighs as if she were painting a corner on a wall that was difficult to get to), she would put the cap back on the tube and then put the tube down on the grass beside the chaise lounge. Then she'd pick up the novel, put on her sunglasses, and read for about ten minutes before she undid her straps. From my window her breasts were visible down to her nipples, which alone were covered by her suit, making it seem that her breasts had no ending, that they merely blended into her skin-colored suit.

. . . I was not getting very far with my trio. I was supposed to be working on the andante, but my mind was going closer to presto. I kept thinking about my dinner with them the night before, how it was I even agreed to go with them. He'd surprised me by knocking on my door. I'd been lying in bed reading and sat up as fast as I could as soon as I heard who it was. Then before I could prepare myself he asked me straight out if I wanted to go with them. Basically, I got flustered and said yes simply because I was afraid he'd see how angry I was. "I'll leave you alone to get dressed," he said. "Can you meet us on the porch in, say, twenty minutes?" Once again the troop leader had me jumping around.

One of my pet peeves is dressing for dinner or dressing up for anything. The whole process just seems so pathetic. You start off looking at yourself naked and then try to improve yourself through matching clothes and makeup. My way of dealing with it is to dress as nondescriptly as possible. Not that I don't have a figure—it's not as good as Linda's but definitely there—I just object to the process of deception, which is what it feels like. Also, because I have dark eyebrows (probably my best feature), I don't really have to wear makeup, although that night for some reason I wore lipstick.

Meanwhile Linda looked like she had stepped out of the pages of *Valley Girl Monthly*. She was all pink and golden, blonde hair curled, baby blue eyes set off with blue eyeliner, pink sequinned dress cut low. Ralph was wearing a red and white Ralph Lauren sports shirt and a navy blue blazer, the approximate color of his

Oldsmobile. This couple was definitely making a statement, but what was it?

Ralph said, "What's the best restaurant in Stockbridge?"

"The Red Lion Inn, I guess."

So naturally we went there. The meal, I admit, was very good, but I was a little nervous the whole time wondering what I was doing with them, what they wanted me for, what game it was they were playing.

Ralph started off talking about his life in New York. He was a successful city planner. Some people were even suggesting he get into politics and he'd been mulling it over. "I'm just his domestic engineer," Linda piped in, as if she had just thought of that phrase that was already an abominable cliché ten years ago.

Right after the main course arrived the topic, as I expected it would, switched to me. Ralph was intent on developing his thesis that I was a frustrated composer just because I was a student at Tanglewood one summer. I felt my cheeks getting flushed, which was doubly embarrassing since I have one of these very bland complexions and my blush is excessively red. Unexpectedly, Linda, who I didn't think was capable of it, leapt to my defense. "Ralph, she's a successful businesswoman, why should she be a frustrated anything?"

His jaw almost snapped shut, but he smiled and tried to assure me that he certainly hadn't meant to imply that.

"The only frustration in your life must come from all the men who've wanted to marry you."

"Ralph," Linda said, and making a little baby fist she punched him in mock anger in his massive chest.

"Whoops," he said, actually looking around the room while he made his eyes look innocent. "Did I say something wrong? Look, Carlin, I'm just clumsily trying to show you how much Linda and I like you, that's all."

I looked at Linda and saw how much she wanted the dinner to go smoothly. So I said thank you and forced myself to smile.

. . . I remember finding it unbearable to be with them when I should have been composing and deciding that as soon as I got home

I'd add to my list, which I knew would eventually settle me down. This is what I wrote later that night in my room.

21 Things I Hate about Ralph Gilbert, All-American City Planner from New York

1. The way he keeps trying to get me to go to the beach with them. I've told him repeatedly I'm not a swimmer, that in five summers at The Terrace I've never even used the pool. Besides, I've always felt two things about the beach: when you take your clothes off and lie down the sun burns you, and when you go in the water next to naked it makes you cold. I've found it's best to stay in your clothes in most circumstances.
2. The neatness of his hair. Neither thick nor thin and always combed in place so that I sometimes think he's wearing a wig.
3. The color of his eyes. No explanation for this. They are pure blue. I hate them.
4. The shape and length of his nose—straight and without imperfection unless the nostrils are too wide. Like the nose of an astronaut.
5. His slightly stocky but otherwise athletic body. He looks like he could do a commercial for Jockey underwear if he lost five pounds.
6. His clothes. He dresses like he's still going to prep school.
7. His constant questions. There's been a shift here. In the beginning the emphasis was on making me confess that my job was meaningless. I was supposed to be this tortured composer lurking in the shadows of Tanglewood. Now he's trying to make me reveal the dark reason why I've never married. Of course, the fact that I'm alone on my vacation completely confounds him. The implication is that he is the solution. But how? In what way? He has never even made a serious pass at me.
8. His horrible slippers.
9. His politics. He actually defended Reagan tonight and bragged about meeting Jack Kemp. Like his wife, it's something he wants to show off. That he's a conservative with a future in politics. Pathetic.

10. The way he shakes hands with me every day, as if God has already blessed his hand and it's perfect. It's worst when it rests on Linda's shoulder. I want to warn her, "There's a fat crab on your shoulder."
11. His passing by every available mirror.
12. His apparently perfect past. Nothing in it seems to bother him. He's always saying to you with his eyes, "Look at me, I've got a clean slate, a past without a blemish. See, I've got nothing to be ashamed of, isn't that wonderful? I've never had a career setback, I've never lost a woman, I always do my job in bed. Everything I have ever done has contributed to all that I am now. Nothing has ever detracted from me. It's all been worth it."
13. His half-assed, overly soapy, quasi-mutant cologne.
14. The way he won't leave me alone at breakfast. (They must wait to hear my door open before leaving for the dining room.) Every morning he comes over to my table to join me, leading Linda by one hand and shaking my hand with the other. As a result I don't digest my food well.
15. The way he makes his wife dress. I'm convinced he orchestrates Linda's wardrobe. I'm sure he thinks her boy-toy clothes give *him* a dash of color, show he's a regular guy. They certainly draw attention to him and make him feel superior, which is his main goal in life anyway.
16. His taste in music. Burt Bachrach, Sinatra, some Boston Pops like the *William Tell Overture*.
17. The way he mentions approximately every twenty minutes his new Audi sitting in the driveway of his home in Westchester.
18. The adolescent amount of noise the two of them produce when they make love. He's a hysterical bass; she's an out-of-control soprano. I'm sure she does it to please him, because nothing on earth makes that much noise naturally. I can actually picture him conducting her with a baton, saying, "Fortissimo, fortissimo!" Of course, I can't complain about it, neither about the vocals nor the thumping of the bed against the wall. What could I say? I have to pretend it doesn't exist, that it's somehow part of my dream life.

19. The way he looked at me last night. Here was the situation: The bathroom on our floor is supposed to be shared by the Gilberts and me. I heard Linda come out of the bathroom, probably still trying to get her makeup right for him. I had to go to the bathroom myself for more utilitarian reasons and in my eagerness I opened my door too soon. She was still in the hallway. I was too stunned to even say hello when I saw her. She was wearing a thin pink nightgown, almost transparent. She probably got it at her local erotica store. She smiled at me and said my name, Carlin, softly, not even with a hello or goodnight before it. I stood still. I could see the dividing line of her rear end as she went into her husband's room and behind her I could see Ralph sitting on the edge of the bed staring out at me with an expression that said, "I've got what everybody wants, but what did you expect? Do you blame me for smiling all the time?"

20. Their impeccably folded, monogrammed, blue-and-pink, his-and-her towels, and related to this the sickening habit they have of calling each other by their non-euphonious initials, R.G. and L.G.

21. His news release at breakfast this morning, right before he started eating his Wheaties, that she's pregnant. I swear it. As if she only exists to prove he's The Masculine Principle itself.

3

We were riding back from Tanglewood in his Oldsmobile. Somehow I wound up in the front seat between him and Linda.

"That was the best concert I've ever been to, Carlin, and I owe it all to you. You're going to make a classical music lover out of me yet. Wasn't that beautiful, Linda?"

"It was beautiful," Linda said.

"Those damn trumpets at the end of the last one were so proud sounding, so exciting. I think we should celebrate. I feel like celebrating."

That meant, of course, that we *would* celebrate. We drove to

Stockbridge, to the Red Lion Inn, and beat the crowds because of a shortcut I knew about. Ralph thanked me profusely.

It had cooled down and the stars were out. The tables outside all had flowers on them and were lit by candles, and for a moment I felt glad to be in the country. Ralph and I decided to drink margaritas. In deference to her condition Linda settled for sipping a Perrier. The Red Lion had a very elaborate bar and the drinks were delicious. After the first round Ralph started talking about his baby.

"I find myself thinking about it in the strangest ways, at the most unexpected times. I keep trying to think of names for it. Of course, it's tough when you don't know the sex yet. Sometimes I feel scared, sure, but mostly I feel happy, like I can't stop smiling. It just gives such an added meaning to things. To tell you the truth, I wish we'd done it earlier, but better late than never."

He finished with his beatific smile intact, and then Linda said, "I really feel this sense of creative fulfillment. I mean I'm not a creative person like you, Carlin, but in a way I feel like this is the ultimate art."

The waitress came with our second round of drinks. She was a pretty kid, who looked about eighteen, and Ralph gave her a long look up and down. I started to think about my abortion (How could I not?), which was only two years ago, and then tried to change the subject. But the subject never got changed that much because we began talking about our parents, and when they asked me about mine I told them that I didn't see them anymore—that we just exchanged cards on holidays. They looked so puzzled and hurt that I tried to explain. "They didn't abuse me or anything, it just didn't work. We couldn't talk without hurting each other, so . . ."

I don't know if it was my parents, or if I was still thinking about my abortion, or what part the drinks played, but I started crying. It was ridiculous—big hot tears falling down my face. Of course I tried to explain it away, and Ralph and Linda reassured me, but it certainly put a damper on our postconcert celebration. They drove me home twenty-five minutes later, making some vapid remarks about all the excitement of the evening. In their own way they seemed freaked out. Crying was obviously not a big part of their world.

4

A half hour after I said goodnight I was sitting up in bed with just the bed lamp on, looking at and hating the score of my trio and realizing I wouldn't finish it—that I'd only finished one piece in the last three years. It felt lifeless, uninspired, like a distant echo of what I wrote ten years ago when I won the scholarship to Tangle-wood. Maybe my parents were right about my composing, I thought, until I remembered that my whole commitment to the store in Cambridge proves that I knew they were right (even if I couldn't stop hating them because of it).

Right in the middle of that cheerful line of thought came two delicate taps on my door. "It's me, Linda. Can I come in?"

"Just a second," I said, jumping out of bed so I could run a brush through my hair, deodorant under my arms, perfume on my neck, mouthwash over my teeth and down my throat, and put a bathrobe over my suddenly shaking body.

Linda looked a little embarrassed when she finally walked in.

"You probably want to be alone but I came to see if you felt like talking."

"Come in. That's really sweet of you. I'm sorry about my outburst."

"Quit apologizing for it. I have them all the time."

I looked surprised. "Really?"

"Sure, what'd you think?"

"I thought that you two were supernaturally well adjusted, I guess."

She gave a little laugh and rolled her sky blue eyes. "Believe me, Ralph and I have had every problem you can think of at one time or another. We're pretty happy now but it took a lot of work and a lot of compromising."

I looked at her closely. She was wearing a pale green pair of pajamas, nothing you could see through this time. It was amazing, she wore something different for him every night. She always smelled unnaturally good too—she was probably wearing a pair of edible undies under her pajamas.

"I'm surprised," I said rather dumbly. "I'm really surprised."

Linda shrugged and looked strangely bemused. "You shouldn't be."

"I just can't imagine what problems you two could have."

"Are you kidding? There was even a time when Ralph was screwing around on me."

"Why'd he do that?"

"That's what I asked him," she said, laughing. "You can imagine how I felt. I nearly left him over it."

I realized we were still standing so I asked if she'd like to sit down and she settled into the swivel chair at my desk. I sat on the edge of my bed and ran my fingers through my hair, wishing it weren't so dully dark and terminally straight, that it could in some mystical way suddenly be prettier.

"So, it's not that what you see isn't true. It's that there's a story behind it that isn't always so pretty or obvious."

I tried to nod sagely. I wanted to ask her hundreds of questions but decided not to. I also wondered if I should tell her about my abortion and my relationship with Ed, a compulsively womanizing medical student who left me—as I always knew he would—a few days after the operation. But I decided to nix that too.

"Well, it's the same with me, as you found out tonight."

"Parents can be a real emotional topic," Linda said, nodding. Then I saw a hard look come over her that I'd never seen before. "I've cried my eyes out over mine many times."

She caught my eye and an intense quiet followed. It was so intense it was as if we'd suddenly been locked together in some kind of freezer. Finally we made a transition to small talk about Tanglewood and Mrs. Blanchard, who owned The Terrace. We talked in this polite, gossipy way for about ten minutes until Linda said she had to go.

"Of course," I said, getting up from the bed.

"Would you play me some of your piece?" she asked, and I felt myself start to shake again.

"How can I?"

"On the piano downstairs. Tomorrow maybe?"

I shrugged my shoulders. "Sure," I said. "If you want."

"I'd love it. Well, goodnight, Carlin. It was great talking with you."

I thanked her for coming and she gave me a hug, pressing me against her for a few seconds.

5

In the morning I went down to the lake before they could get me for breakfast. I hadn't slept the night before and I just couldn't face them. There was a small public beach about a quarter mile from The Terrace. For some crazy reason I climbed to the top of the life-guard's chair and stared out at the unruffled lake. A mist still covered most of it, hiding Tanglewood beach and the monastery in the hills, as well as much of the island to the left.

I decided I had to sort out the questions swirling inside me to gain some perspective. Since I didn't bring any paper, I did it in my mind alone.

1. What did they want from me? Why did it feel like a trick, a setup? They must want me to sleep with them but what would I say, really, if they tried?

2. Last night I couldn't deny that I would have slept with Linda. That certainly confused things. I'd had very little sex with women in my life and no sex at all with anyone since my relationship with Ed. Actually, I thought that during the vacation I'd sort out my feelings about men. I thought the thing with women was just an aberration, something I did when I was extremely lonely. Not that sex was a major priority in my life, but it wasn't so minor that it didn't have to be addressed sometime.

3. How much would I risk to have Linda? And what about Ralph? They had to be in this together—they were like a doubles team, the way they kept switching positions, backing each other up, maneuvering me.

4. Of course this could all be a rationalization because I didn't want to risk *anything* for Linda. When had I ever risked anything for what I really cared about? How hard did I really try with my parents or Ed or my music even? It was true that I'd always succeeded best with things that weren't close to me.

5. Why had I let them become so important to me anyway? Why did I react so strongly to them? Our vacations were both nearly over.

In a few days they'd be gone. Then there'd be a letter or two, or a postcard more likely; then a Christmas card, a phone call on New Year's Day; then time would just ship them off and it wouldn't matter. None of it. How could people stand what Time was? Why didn't more people go crazy?

6

The sun came through the half-raised shade and the room seemed to shake a little, like a big square of jelly prodded by a fork. First I panicked, as if the light stripped me of my dignity, revealing my face to be all whiteness and emptiness.

I kept walking stiffly but apparently going forward toward the piano. When I sat down on the bench I could feel my period coming on, and I wondered vaguely why I'd put on my most expensive skirt. Why make this more than it was?

I closed my eyes for a second and saw an image of my parents looking at me with their characteristic hardness in their eyes, in fact, their eyes were identical, as if they were sharing each others' eyes, or four eyes were sharing them. I played my first piano sonata (my opus 1) straight through, a little too fast and with a couple of fluffs, but okay under the circumstances. Ralph and Linda applauded, so did Mrs. Blanchard, who'd come in from the kitchen, and a kid with a mole on his cheek the size of a dime, and a man who was wearing glasses and looked like the kid's father.

I'd already told the Gilberts exactly what I'd be playing and in what order so I wouldn't have to do any talking, but I couldn't help saying, "A little derivative of Prokofiev at times, but I was only eighteen when I wrote it."

Then I played a piano version of the third movement of my string quartet. That took about seven minutes. It was more dissonant, actually it's pretty much atonal, but there was still applause at the end. A few more guests (who were talking a little in the beginning of the piece) were now sitting on the red velvet sofa next to Mrs. Blanchard.

I ended by playing the first and, at that point, only movement of my piano trio. By then I was strangely relaxed and it went crisply, without a hitch.

There was more applause. When it ended the audience sat waiting as if I were supposed to make a speech. Instinctively I walked toward the Gilberts and Ralph jumped up from his straight-back chair (he was leaning forward, eyes riveted on me, during the whole concert) and gave me a dramatic hug and kiss. I averted my head enough so that it landed on my cheek. Linda—all smiles—hugged me and kissed me on the other cheek.

I began exchanging pleasantries with the other guests (it turned out the kid with the mole wanted to be a pianist) when Ralph grabbed my hand and said, "Come on, we're going to celebrate. I want to go to the beach with my favorite composer in the world. Come on, Chopin, get in your suit, I won't take no for an answer."

I felt a mixture of confusion and relief and then a kind of passivity. I guess I was more exhausted than anything.

7

. . .We ended up going to the same beach I went to that morning. It was late in the afternoon, but the sun was still strong and there were still a number of people on the beach. Ralph took an army blanket and a frisbee out of the car. He was wearing a short blue bathing suit, Linda was wearing her pink two-piece, and I was in my 1950s-style one-piece. I also wore a long white shirt that I'd gotten from my father. Ralph and Linda lay next to each other on the blanket and I lay next to Linda. They kept complimenting me on the concert, but after a few minutes Ralph make a joke about my wearing so many clothes. I turned over on my stomach and mumbled something into the sand.

"Come on, Frosty, what gives?" he said. "We came here to go swimming."

"Don't listen to Wild Bill Hickok," Linda said.

"What's that?" he said.

"Come on, Wild Bill, I'll go swimming with you."

He asked me to join them again, then Linda made another wise remark and he ended up running after her into the water.

I turned and watched them laughing and splashing each other. I watched them swim out to the second raft and waved to them as they went down the slide together. Suddenly I realized that they weren't plotting to sleep with me at all, neither one of them. It was a strange feeling and I didn't know if I was happy or sad.

Meanwhile they were swimming around the raft and out of sight, probably to play some love games in the water. I closed my eyes and kind of napped for a few minutes. When I got up I started to walk over to the snack bar to buy a fudgesicle but before I got there Ralph and Linda came running in from the water, their suits gleaming in the sunlight.

"Carlin, hey, wait up, Wild Bill has to tell you something." He suddenly turned serious, the same way he did when he talked about Reagan.

"We made a big decision behind the raft out there. Boy or girl, we're going to name our baby Carlin. See, we love your name and we wanted you to be the first to know."

"No joking?"

"Scout's honor."

"What can I say, I'm touched."

We were all quiet and serious for a few seconds. Then Ralph suggested we play frisbee and ran to the blanket to get it. We followed him up the hill past the picnic tables where there was a clearing in the grassy section of the beach. We made some casual throws then assumed our positions about fifty feet away from each other. After a few minutes it got hot, so I took my shirt off. Ralph made a joke and then resumed throwing. Soon our throws got synchronized and there was very little running. The frisbee was white with a gold center. While it floated it looked like a little sun. Round after round went by effortlessly, with no mistakes. I kept concentrating on the frisbee and soon the rest of the beach began to fade as though it were part of the shadows and only the three of us playing were out in the sun. I could see them making their moves so clearly, though I couldn't say for certain how many feet away from me they were, or whether we still formed a triangle or any kind of design. Even the space between us blurred as if it were imaginary. I just kept my eyes on the frisbee, catching and throwing, and feeling the sun. For a moment I thought, "At last, this is paradise."

The Victims

It was twenty-two years ago that my eighth-grade baseball coach decided I should be his starting shortstop instead of Andrew Auer. As he announced the starting line-up a half hour before game time, I looked at Andy four seats away from me on the bench and saw an expression I've only seen since in children who have suffered a disappointment so great it doesn't seem comprehensible. I think it was that expression more than anything else that encouraged me to become his friend. Maybe I felt he was someone who would never hurt me. Besides, at that time I could appreciate his sensitivity while luxuriating in a secret sense of superiority. In school we were about even, but besides beating him out for shortstop, I lived in a large house with professionally successful parents, while Andy was the only child of a young divorcée who lived in one of the less-fashionable parts of Newton.

For the next four years our friendship flourished. We seemed to discover the same things at the same time. By our junior year in high school I would listen to Thelonious Monk or to Mahler symphonies with him, and we'd share our first attempts at writing poetry or fiction. Outside of my family, Andy was the most important person in my life. He was almost unfailingly compassionate. Even when I lost my virginity before he did, he forgave me. He became especially important to me then, because I could never confide anything like that to my sister or parents.

But a year later when he lost his, I was considerably less charitable. Andy didn't simply lose his virginity with another teenager, after all, he had an affair with a thirty-one-year-old German woman named Lizette who seemed shockingly attractive to me. How had this happened? It was such an outrageous coup I couldn't comprehend it. She was a former model from Munich and a divorcée, while Andy was a Jewish virgin and a second-string shortstop. They kept their trysts secret from everyone except me, meeting once or twice a week in her apartment for an entire summer. I was so shaken I even told my mother about it, who assured me that I, too, would have many triumphs in my life and that I should "let him have his."

Finally Lizette went back to Germany, but no sooner had she gone than I discovered that Andy scored eighty points higher than I did on his college boards, and that despite my parents paying for two years of private school for me, he got accepted by a more prestigious college. Still, Andy was far from insufferable about it. He was in his anarchistic phase then, very much under the influence of Henry Miller, and assured me all he wanted to do was to become a great writer. I somehow wasn't surprised to see him knocking on my front door four months after Antioch started, having hitchhiked all the way from Ohio and vowing never to return. I was surprised, however, that Roberta, his mother, didn't force him to go back. I never knew precisely what her reaction was, only that that year he stayed at home with her.

The next year, Andy decided he had to live in New York. Newton, in fact all of Massachusetts, was "too small and provincial" for a writer with his "concern for the world." As a concession to his mother he agreed to enroll at Columbia. This time he stayed for about a year and a half before quitting in a rage. I never learned exactly what went wrong. He was doing well academically (his mother said he was offered a university scholarship) but he began fighting with his professors or intermittently losing his concentration in class. At night he'd suffer from insomnia. His mother called me and pleaded with me to talk him into going back to school. "Marty, you're his best friend, he'll listen to you. His uncle is going to wash his hands of the whole thing and then he'll never be able to get a degree."

I called Andy and gave him all the standard arguments (which I only half believed) for finishing college, but he wasn't convinced.

He stayed in New York reading and writing and "exploring life," supported by his mother and her brother.

"If he doesn't straighten out, he'll never get a job. His mother can't support him his whole life," my mother said. But getting a job, despite occasional threats from his mother and uncle, was literally the last thing on Andy's mind. Not only did he still worship Henry Miller, he'd discovered Gertrude Stein's entire "lost generation." It was both the most natural and imperative thing in the world, as he saw it, to escape "the absurd contradictions and crass materialism of America," and to move to Paris. Now his uncle did stop contributing money but in a strange turnaround Roberta defended her son's ambitions, fought with her brother, and told him not to bother calling her again. Then she left her secretarial job at a Boston hospital and began selling life insurance. She didn't enjoy her new work with its increased responsibilities, for Roberta was not a person who reacted well to pressure, but she felt she had to do it for Andy. Eventually she grew quite adept. For the next three years she was able to support him in his studio apartment in Paris. "I believe in him, Marty," she would say to me whenever I questioned her. "You know how brilliant he is. Isn't he brilliant? Isn't he as talented as anyone his age?"

"He's very bright."

"All right then. He's going to make it. He'll support himself from writing. Look at Norman Mailer, look at Gore Vidal. It can happen. He'll do it. He just needs some peace of mind to develop. He says Europe's the place, he must know. Look at Hemingway and Fitzgerald. It will happen."

At that time I had finally left Newton, and was going to graduate school at New York University. School wasn't easy for me but I was a steady, if unspectacular, student. When my parents sometimes complained about how expensive my tuition was I'd feel the same envy for Andy's life that I used to feel when he was sleeping with Lizette. But it wasn't envy alone I felt. I also admired him and felt he deserved his life in a way I never could. Secretly, I'd conceded a number of things to him. He had a greater intellectual curiosity than I did. I struggled to pass my foreign language requirement at N.Y.U., but he could speak fluent French and German and was teaching himself Italian. For every book I'd read, he'd read two; not only literary books but philosophy, psychology, even books about painting or sculpture. Why *did* he need school? He also had an intensity, a generosity of spirit that I didn't. By comparison I felt petty and spiteful, even ordinary. It's true that by conventional standards I might have been considered better looking but Andy had raven black hair, in fact the blackest hair and greenest eyes I'd ever seen. Even his personality made a bigger impact on people. He had a better sense of humor and was more trusting. People gravitated toward him and seemed ambivalent about me. No wonder he was able to get his way with his mother, even at the expense of her breaking off relations with her brother.

Of course, there were my undeniable advantages over Andy—my family's financial success and status, the sad fact that he hadn't had any contact with his father since he was eight. But more often than not the absence of a father seemed to me one more romantic detail about Andy. It gave his life, like Gatsby's, a certain self-created quality.

While I always thought Andy remarkable, I only rarely thought I was. Maybe that's why I left graduate school after I got my master's to teach in a prep school in western Massachusetts. I was twenty-three then and felt uncomfortable taking any more money from my parents. Meanwhile, Andy and I continued to exchange letters from Northfield, Mass., to Paris. In his letters he always seemed on the verge of a major breakthrough in his work. He said he was friendly with Michel Foucault, that he was contemplating going to the Sorbonne, that he was writing a novel, a screenplay, and a book on aesthetics, that he'd slept with Ingmar Bergman's daughter and a certain prominent American critic whose name I can't mention. I began to suspect he might be exaggerating but I couldn't be sure. With Andy anything seemed possible, there was never a way to prove him wrong.

That summer I visited him in Paris for two weeks. I must have been very excited since it was the first time I'd been to Europe, but what I chiefly remember is the awe, the infinite hopefulness in his face as he told me about his new life. I think we were walking in the Tuileries, though we could just as easily have been in his studio. It is his face, the excitement in his green eyes that I am sure of, as he told me he'd increased his "overall grasp of literature exponentially. The people that I've met here are incredible, the entire ambiance— it's become my spiritual home. I only wish you could stay longer."

After a passionate description of his French female conquests he told me that his mother was now seriously involved with a very wealthy Boston businessman. Roberta was only eighteen when Andy was born, twenty-six when she was divorced. Since then she'd only dated a handful of colorless men. Although she was extremely youthful and attractive, I'd somehow never imagined her with any- one but Andy. I pressed him for more details but he held up his hands to stop me. "I can only talk about it so much," he said, forming a short space between his thumb and index finger. "It could mean so much to her but I just don't want to say more until some- thing definite happens."

Andy's revelation dwarfed whatever else I did in Paris, and I returned to Boston wondering how much of what he'd told me was true. Within a week, Roberta took me into her confidence and told me about "the special man" in her life, Benjamin Walters, who had invested prophetically in communication systems, and was indeed a wealthy man. Not only was he rich, but he was investing in Broad- way shows and other theatrical endeavors which put him in touch with people that Roberta, who'd never been out of Newton, had previously only read about. Suddenly she was eating dinner with these stars and accompanying Benjamin for quick trips to Las Vegas or Hollywood. It was clearly the adventure of her life.

Eventually I had dinner with them in the more expensive apart- ment she'd moved into in Beacon Hill. Benjamin Walters was over- weight, shy, preoccupied with his work, but he did exude a certain gruff charm. At times he looked and acted a bit like a New England Broderick Crawford. The morning after her dinner she called me to ask me my impressions, not so much of Benjamin but of how serious I thought he was about her. It was a question she would ask me in many different ways over the next three years. Of course, I never gave her an absolute answer. I was always embarrassed, although also a little flattered when she asked my opinion. Generally I tried to encourage her because when she felt encouraged she'd be happy and she was wonderful to talk to when her basic optimism resurfaced.

Andy, meanwhile, had made some important career decisions. He'd abandoned his attempts to write novels or screenplays and concentrated instead on what he was best at, literary and social criticism. He began publishing book reviews in literary quarterlies, then longer and more theoretical essays. Within three years he was occasionally reviewing for *The New Republic* and *The Nation*.

I felt competitive and a trifle envious, though, of course, I was happy for him too. Besides, I had distractions of my own, principally a series of short, intense love affairs. As for my career, I had managed to publish a few stories in little magazines. (I thought of them, at the time, as proof of the important creative distinction between me and Andy. So what if they appeared in magazines with circulations under a thousand. They proved I was "an artist," didn't they?) I'd also left the private school in the country and become an English instructor in a junior college in Boston. What I was concentrating on chiefly was getting tenure. I saw that as the necessary first step to anything else I wanted from life, so I methodically plugged away at it. That's how it was in those days: I was plugging away after tenure, Roberta was plugging away after Benjamin Walters, while Andy was pursuing the legacy of Edmund Wilson and making impressive progress.

Finally, after three years Roberta got discouraged, then angry that Benjamin wouldn't marry her.

"He says he's got a hang-up about marriage, but I think he's just a cheapskate. He doesn't want to part with any of his big bucks. I don't care for him myself; it's Andy I'm worried about."

"Andy seems to be doing fine, he's flourishing."

"Marty, I still have to support him. I may always have to help him."

"At the rate he's going he'll probably be making his own 'big bucks' from writing," I said, surprised that I was assuming the argument she usually used to defend Andy's life.

"Maybe you should give Benjamin, you know, an ultimatum of some kind," I said softly. Roberta ran her fingers through her own raven black hair, only slightly flecked with a few silver streaks. Her eyes were also sharp and green; she looked like a feminine version of Andy.

"I probably should, but the truth is, Marty, I'm afraid he'd say no. . . . Anyway, he's promised to always take care of me."

A few months later Andy moved back to New York to capitalize on his initial successes. I think we were both so busy with our careers that in some ways we had less contact than when he was in Europe. Also, I had become seriously involved with Lianne, an assistant art professor at my college, and within a few months we were virtually living together. During his last visit to Boston I only found time to have one lunch with Andy. Every time I spoke I ended up mentioning Lianne, as if my mouth took a compulsive delight in pronouncing her name. When I asked Andy if he was seeing anyone he alluded to his usual list of glamorous one-night stands and then changed the subject.

I felt guilty for not spending more time with him during his visit and a month later, after a new review of his on Samuel Beckett had been published, I wrote him a long congratulatory letter.

Andy wrote me back eight pages. Typically, his references ranged from Proust to Heidegger to Miles Davis to the Abstract Expressionists. But it was the confessional part near the end that I still remember:

> You praise me for having so much to say about Beckett, but there is so much more I want to say, so much more inside me that I need to utter and I feel thwarted and ashamed that I still can't fashion it into decent prose. If only I could write poetry! Besides the desire to write something I am not disgusted with, I want only three things in life: happiness for my mother who has sacrificed everything for me; happiness for my friends—most of all for you since you are my most treasured friend; and a little taste of the love you have found with Lianne. I realize now that I have not yet been able to fall in love.

I decided to never let too much time pass without seeing Andy. That summer he was in Boston a lot and I would see him two or three times a week. He and I and Lianne would sometimes go to the movies together or walk around Harvard Square, but I was careful not to let him spend too much time with her. It wasn't that I didn't trust them—it was just easier for me to deal with them separately, perhaps because each required such an intense and different kind of attention. I also realized that I didn't understand Andy's sexuality— it was so ferocious yet detached, like a caged lion that was only temporarily calm. He was constantly evoking this or that starlet (usually European ones) as the apotheosis of beauty or sex appeal but the only woman I'd ever seen him express any strong emotion for was his mother. It was Roberta who could provoke his temper as no one else could, Roberta who could still induce his screaming fits the same as when he was an eighth grader, and it was Roberta whom he would still unabashedly smother with kisses, even in my presence.

One weekend in July, Lianne went home to visit her parents and I went to Roberta's apartment to meet Andy. We were planning to go to a literary party of some kind. When I arrived Andy was still dressing, and I saw Benjamin Walters sitting on Roberta's sofa. Corpulent, slow moving, he was wrapped in his dark blue suit like a mummy. We exchanged five minutes of awkward small talk while Roberta, dressed in a tight-fitting pink gown that showed off her slim figure, fluttered around him like a cocktail waitress. That evening she was obviously going to cook him another dinner.

"You know, I can't stand him," Andy said to me in his car as we searched for the party in Cambridge. "If it weren't for my mother I probably would have punched him out a couple of times by now."

"But he seems to make your mother happy. I've never seen her so animated."

"Of course, and that's everything to me," he said, as his voice softened. "But it's ironic that the love of my mother's life should be such a bloated, petty, ignorant, self-involved, penurious nouveau riche. . . ." He searched for more adjectives and then started to laugh. "I wish for two minutes I could be Marcel Proust just to once and for all do verbal justice to Benjamin. The point is, I could forgive him for being so culturally bankrupt, but he has the chutzpah to lecture me and my mother about how I should get a job and work for him in his business. The man is actually trying to parent me. Meanwhile, if he'd only marry my mother she could finally stop working for once in her life, but he's too goddamn cheap to marry her and he's been sleeping with her for four years now."

"Still, you know, he might marry her and you should try to be nice to him. It can only benefit you."

"Believe me he *will* marry her. And within one year after their marriage I'll launch the most important literary magazine in America since *The Dial*. Who knows, since he has millions, I may even start a small publishing company that will only publish books of real quality."

As if sensing the pang of envy I was feeling, he quickly added, "Of course, Marty, you'll leave that little college where they're mistreating you and be my partner."

At the party there were a number of attractive women. I told Andy that I was being faithful to Lianne and that he should go after whomever he wanted. But Andy found something wrong with every one of them. One of them was a little too plump, another looked too Jewish, a third, who was obviously pretty, he claimed had "no hips or breasts, she might turn out to be a boy."

We ended up drinking a lot at the party and then walking along the Charles River afterward to sober up. "If Benjamin ever double-crossed my mother I think I'd be justified in killing him, don't you?" he said as we walked past a series of couples making out on the benches or on the grass by the river.

"What are you saying, are you serious?"

"You don't agree, you think that's sick?"

"I think you're too close to your mother. Can't you find a girl-friend, instead of all those one-night things?"

"You're right. It's because I know she needs me; she's given everything to me."

"But she has someone. She has Benjamin and you're still alone. . . ."

"You're right, Marty. As soon as I get back to New York I'm going to work on it. I'll have a girlfriend within two weeks."

A few hours later, at two or three in the morning, I was asleep in my apartment when the phone rang. Andy's voice was saying words to me I could scarcely absorb.

"Something unbelievable happened. Benjamin had a heart attack. I'm calling you from the hospital. My mother's in shock."

I went to Benjamin's funeral with Roberta and Andy. Roberta cried throughout the service and then intermittently during the reception at Benjamin's brother's home. Andy was by her side every moment, his face rigid with a kind of heightened alertness.

A few days later it was determined that Benjamin hadn't left a will. As the next of kin, Benjamin's brother put in a claim for the whole estate and offered Roberta $10,000. He had grossly underestimated her. Of course, at this time palimony suits were still unheard of, and in all those years Roberta had never technically lived with Benjamin. But Roberta's claim was that Benjamin had verbally promised her his estate in lieu of marrying her, and that she had faithfully rendered to him the services of a wife.

A month later, Benjamin's brother claimed to have located a homemade will leaving him everything. The controversy wound up in court and dragged on for a year, with handwriting experts contradicting each other, with appeals and counterappeals. I was one of the witnesses who testified for Roberta. It was peculiar; I thought she was probably telling the truth most of the time, but the mere participation in an attempt to get someone's money made me feel a little like I was committing a crime.

Since Benjamin's death Andy had moved back with his mother. Like Roberta, he became obsessed with the details of the trial. He stopped writing, and even read very little. He was too nervous to attend the various hearings. Of course it was impossible to get much pleasure from his company in those days, but in some ways our friendship was stronger than ever. Not only did he and Roberta need me as a confidant about the twists and turns of their case, but I needed them as well. I was having my own crisis. Lianne and I had broken up (I'd found out that she'd slept with someone in her department) and the pain of adjusting to living alone was worse than I'd anticipated. Also I found out I was coming up for tenure a year earlier than I'd expected and was very anxious about it. My own rate of publishing had fallen well behind my expectations. In short, listening to Roberta's and Andy's monologues about their case (as well as their occasional epiphanies about all the things they could do when they finally got their money) seemed a small price to pay for some genuine empathy for my loss of Lianne, and my troubles with tenure.

Another year passed before Roberta was finally awarded her settlement. It was far less than Andy and she had dreamed of, but it was more than a half-million dollars. I had meanwhile managed to postpone the decision on my tenure for another year. What better time was there to finally discuss with Andy our long-planned magazine which we both needed to revitalize our careers?

A month after the Auers won their case, when they'd returned from a short vacation in Europe, I invited Andy to dinner at a small French restaurant in Harvard Square. Perhaps because we hadn't talked about the magazine in a long time, or because I wanted it so much, I led up to it gradually. I waited until we had our main course and were on our second bottle of wine before I mentioned how much I needed to publish to get tenure. Andy stared past me and gave me a rather perfunctorily sympathetic nod. I switched to another approach and began railing against those young critics in Andy's field who were publishing everywhere and whom we both knew to be mediocrities. Again he didn't take the hint.

"So when are we going to start working on our magazine?" I suddenly blurted out.

Andy focused his eyes on me darkly.

"About the magazine you have to understand something, Marty. It's not my money, it's my mother's. She deserves so many things and now she has a chance to get some of them. She's going to decide how every penny is spent."

"Of course, I understand. But you could ask her. I mean, it's only $5,000 or $10,000 we're talking about, initially."

"Maybe if we'd gotten the whole estate, but now? No, I won't even ask her."

"I don't understand. What have we been talking about the past four or five years?"

"I don't care about the past. My mother and I are starting a new life."

"But . . ."

"No more buts," he screamed, slamming his fist on the table. The veins stood out in his thin forehead the way they did when he'd have a temper tantrum playing baseball as a kid, or else fighting with Roberta.

"Is that why you testified at the trial? Is that why you've been my 'friend' all these years, because you want your cut? You want to rob me too, like Benjamin and his brother, and the courts, and my father. I'm nauseated. I never want to see you again!"

He got up from the table and left the restaurant. A few minutes later I went home, shaken. During that sleepless first night, I was sure he would call and apologize. I'd seen him have these temporary rages before and then become profoundly apologetic an hour or two later. But the call didn't come. Then I thought he'd write me or that Roberta would contact me, but neither happened and soon a week had passed.

I began to wonder if I were all the things he accused me of. Who had betrayed whom? Who was the victim, Andy or me? Yes, I had wanted to do a magazine, but I'd never made a secret of it, and it was Andy who'd suggested it first. Would I have testified for Roberta if there were no magazine involved? Of course. Would I also have listened so religiously to all his anxieties if there were no hope of my benefiting from it? I was still sure I would have. After all, we'd been friends since childhood.

Another week went by. I almost called him many times but my own pride and sense of justice stopped me. I finally told my parents what had happened and my father shook his head and walked out of the room. My mother had a few things to say, however.

"They're the schemers, they're the opportunists. They're what they accuse you of being. I say good riddance. Andy's gotten a free ride through life. He's just jealous of you because you work like a normal person and don't live off your parents. If you ask me, they're both *meshuga*, and you're lucky to be rid of them."

But I didn't feel so lucky and I finally wrote Andy a long conciliatory letter. He didn't answer me and when I phone him a week later I learned that they'd already moved.

Four years went by, maybe five. I had new love affairs, new disappointments. I didn't get tenure, but I managed to get a series of one-year teaching jobs near Boston. I published a few more stories. Through the grapevine I heard Andy and his mother had moved to Lexington, then to New Hampshire, then to Cape Cod. I was hurt by

Andy, but I felt so clearly wronged that it grew easier to forget him. Eventually, I only thought about him once a week or so, as if he were a relative who had died years ago. I never saw his name in print again (although I instinctively avoided those magazines most likely to publish him), which made forgetting him still easier.

Shortly after Christmas each year, the Modern Language Association holds its national convention. Although a number of academics present various papers, the main purpose of the convention is for college English chairs to interview various candidates for their departments. Last year's convention was in New York, and I considered myself fortunate to have secured two interviews, although one was for a junior college, and the other (which was a "tenure track" job) was for a college in an obscure town in Arkansas.

After my last interview I walked out of the Hilton and began replaying the sequence of questions and answers that had just occurred five minutes before. It was bitter cold outside. The sky looked drained, as if it were too depleted of energy to send out any color that day. For no particular reason I headed east. When the wind blew it seemed to cut into my face. Around Second Avenue and 55th Street I stopped at a red light. Someone had called out my name loudly and shrilly two or three times. I turned and saw Roberta.

She was still strikingly pretty, in a white fur coat with her carefully coiffured black hair, and her green eyes under a stylish pair of sunglasses. Physically she had aged, if at all, in very subtle ways.

"Don't turn away, Marty. Come on, give me a hug. Let's forget the past, we can forgive each other, can't we?"

We embraced and at Roberta's suggestion walked into a nearby coffee shop. Once at our table we continued our small talk for another minute or two. I noticed that she looked a little sad when I told her I'd just come from a job interview.

"So how's Andy?" I finally said.

"You'll see him tonight. I'm cooking him dinner in his loft in Soho."

"Are you . . . where are you living now?"

Roberta told me matter-of-factly about her apartment in Sutton

Place but a moment later she clutched my arm just above my wrist and said, "Promise me you'll come tonight, it will mean so much to him."

"Of course, I'll try."

"No, you have to promise. Marty, you've got to forgive him." She took off her sunglasses and wiped away a few tears. "These last five years have been a nightmare."

"I'd just heard that you moved a lot."

"You've heard of the 'wandering Jews,' right? We're setting a record."

She listed the places they'd lived in that I already knew about, and two other places that I didn't.

"What's the trouble, why do you keep moving?"

"He makes me move. One place is too isolated, the other is too noisy. He has problems now, Marty, he's not the way you remember."

"He's not working?"

"He says he's writing but I can't be sure. We wasted four years on a lousy psychiatrist—he should rot in hell. He put Andy on all the wrong medication. But now he's found a new doctor who he thinks is God. Andy can still turn it around. You know how talented he is."

"He never got a job," I said, immediately regretting my words.

"He can do it with his writing. Look at Truman Capote, look at John Updike. They never taught, they didn't need degrees. If he were healthy and writing he'd be making a million dollars. Marty, just promise me you'll come tonight. Here, I'll write down the address."

I went back to my hotel, dazed by my meeting with Roberta and the prospect of seeing Andy in just a few hours. On my bed I closed my eyes and saw a series of pictures of my past with Andy, one at a time like paintings in a gallery: Andy in his Paris studio, Andy walking out of the movies with Lianne and me, Andy like a sentinel at Benjamin's funeral, Andy on the bench at the baseball game twenty years ago.

I forced myself to get up—I had to buy them a bottle of wine, after all, and I'd fallen asleep in my suit. Roberta was probably exaggerating about Andy's condition. Like my own mother, she was hopelessly melodramatic.

Andy lived on Spring Street in one of the more elegant parts of Soho. He shook my hand with a quizzical but benign smile on his face.

"I'm sorry about what happened between us."

"Forget it," I said quickly.

"I guess we're both nervous," he said, as he led me into the living room. Waving at me from a distance, Roberta immediately walked into a bedroom and left us alone. Andy was wearing jeans and a sport shirt and I made a joke about showing up in a suit. He laughed and handed me a glass of champagne. I noticed that his hair had receded even more than mine, and that he now had as many crow's feet around his eyes as Roberta.

"Let me show you the loft," he said, walking ahead of me. The walls were covered with paintings, prints, and photographs. Some of them, like a print by Pollock or Chagall, were of real value. He gave me a brief history of each picture but I forgot most of what he said. Where there weren't paintings, there were high white shelves completely filled with books.

"How many books do you have?" I said.

"Guess?"

"I don't know. It looks like a library."

"Five thousand, all alphabetically arranged," he said, beaming with pride. He continued his walking tour, stopping periodically to give me the history of a lamp or quilt. "I always wanted to live here, some incredible people live around me, you know," and he rattled off a list of art world luminaries. "They're here now and in the summer they go to the Hamptons. By the way, this summer my mother's going to buy a place there. She's already trying to sell the Sutton Place apartment."

We continued walking slowly in circles around the loft. I realized he was no longer nervous, but the angry wit, the edge to his personality, was missing.

We finally stopped walking and sat down on a couch by a window.

"I'm sorry I didn't answer your letter," he said softly. "I don't know how much my mother told you but I've been having some troubles. . . the past few years.''

"She mentioned you were seeing a doctor.''

"Marty, I'm on a lot of medication. Thirteen different pills a day.''

"What's the matter?''

He smiled ironically and shrugged his shoulders.

"Maybe you shouldn't spend so much time with your mother?''

"Oh, no, I'd be dead without her. I owe her everything. The only thing is she's never been able to enjoy her money. I mean, how can she be happy as long as I'm sick? My sickness is keeping her from everything she wants,'' he said sadly, with a strange smile on his lips.

"So you've been living with her?''

"This is the first time we've been apart in five years. It's an experiment. My doctor ordered it.''

Roberta came out of the bedroom in a bright blue skirt with a matching sweater and began making her final preparations for dinner. Andy signaled to me and we changed the subject. But it had been so long since the three of us had talked, and even longer since we'd talked about anything but the trial, that it was awkward. When Roberta sent Andy to the store to get some last-minute things for dinner, I knew she was going to take advantage of her time alone with me to talk about Andy.

As soon as he shut the elevator door Roberta led me by the arm to the sofa by the window.

"So what do you think about Andy?''

"I don't know what to say.''

"How bad does he seem to you?''

"He seems pretty down on himself.''

"Marty, his ego's on the floor. He's a thirty-five-year-old man who's never accomplished anything in his life. Think how he feels.''

"So the main thing is that he's stopped writing, that's the main symptom?''

"Marty, he hasn't been with a woman in years. He sleeps twelve hours a day and he lists.''

"Lists?''

"He has hundreds of rituals that he goes through every day. His doctor calls it 'listing.' "

"You mean writing things down compulsively?"

"Sometimes it's that, other times it's just in his mind. His doctor calls it a 'rage for order.' "

"So what do his doctors say has caused all this?"

"They contradict each other. One says it's congenital, another says something else. Between all the doctors and the moving I'm starting to go through my capital. I'm still trying to sell our house in New Hampshire. The real estate market's collapsed. I'm losing so much money with all this buying and selling I'd be ashamed to tell you."

"So stop moving."

"I shouldn't listen to him, I know. I tell him the problem's inside him, it's not where he's living."

"You gave up your job too?"

"I couldn't work. He'd call me four or five times a day at my office, every time he had a problem. It was impossible . . . Marty, you've got to be his friend again. Stay the night. He needs to know that you're his friend again."

"Of course . . ."

Roberta was an exquisite cook. Her chicken crêpes were so delicious that we all became engrossed in our dinner, without worrying about safe topics of conversation. By the time we got to her chocolate mousse and the champagne, we began reminiscing about our high school years and even our grammar school baseball team. Andy grew especially animated and told a couple of jokes. For a few minutes he was just like his old self. But when Roberta warned him not to drink too much because of his medication he glared at her for a moment and turned somber.

A few minutes later he got up from the table and sat down in a chair in the middle of the loft and turned on the television. I continued talking with Roberta, quietly but ineffectually. Every half-minute she'd turn her head and look at Andy. A little later we heard him snoring.

"This happens every night. He sits in the chair, turns on the TV, and in half an hour he falls asleep."

I noticed that it was only 9:30.

"Well, I may as well go to sleep too," she said, yawning. "In a couple of hours he'll wake up and go to his room. I'll fix up the couch for you by the window."

"You're sure you don't want the couch? It's much bigger."

"No, no," she said, handing me my sheets and pillow. "I always sleep on that little bed in the living room when I visit him."

A half-hour later Roberta and Andy were snoring in unison. I lay on the couch unable to read or sleep, feeling trapped and abandoned. I couldn't remember the last time I'd tried to sleep so early. When I turned off the bed lamp I started to think about Lianne. When that got too painful I began reviewing my job interviews and I thought of all the vain and foolish things I'd done to try to get hired at schools I already had contempt for.

I got up and fixed myself a drink. Mother and son were still snoring loudly. In the vastness of the loft it echoed like a bizarre kind of church music. My mother was right, they are *mechuga*, I thought. But when I lay down again I began to feel sorry for them. They're the victims, I said to myself, answering my question of five years ago.

I finally fell asleep, but a few hours later I woke up from a nightmare that involved both my parents and Lianne. My heart was pounding and I could hear someone pacing in the loft. When I shifted the venetian blinds there was just enough light for me to see Andy walking. I saw him making some vague and frenzied gestures in the air, like a conductor frantically cuing his wayward orchestra. I realized he was doing one of his rituals, and I watched him continue his pattern of gestures in a slow, methodical circle around his loft. When his walk brought him a few feet in front of the couch I felt an impulse to get up and stop him. I almost said, "Stop pacing, or listing, or worrying. Whatever it is, just stop. Lie down in bed, next to me if you have to, but just stop."

Christ, I'm starting to lose it, I thought, as Andy began walking away from me toward the TV. Then I remembered that in my nightmare Lianne, whom I'd been kissing, had turned into Andy. I forced myself to analyze the dream for a minute, because I always analyzed the dreams I could remember.

"So what if Andy and I have always been a little in love with each other, and with our mothers too, and with all the wrong people. Just a lot of bad career moves."

I said this in the jokingly cynical tone of voice I usually used in talking to myself, but tears came to my eyes anyway.

"We're all victims," I said, but softly enough so that Andy couldn't hear me.

ILLINOIS SHORT FICTION

Crossings by Stephen Minot
A Season for Unnatural Causes by Philip F. O'Connor
Curving Road by John Stewart
Such Waltzing Was Not Easy by Gordon Weaver

Rolling All the Time by James Ballard
Love in the Winter by Daniel Curley
To Byzantium by Andrew Fetler
Small Moments by Nancy Huddleston Packer

One More River by Lester Goldberg
The Tennis Player by Kent Nelson
A Horse of Another Color by Carolyn Osborn
The Pleasures of Manhood by Robley Wilson, Jr.

The New World by Russell Banks
The Actes and Monuments by John William Corrington
Virginia Reels by William Hoffman
Up Where I Used to Live by Max Schott

The Return of Service by Jonathan Baumbach
On the Edge of the Desert by Gladys Swan
Surviving Adverse Seasons by Barry Targan
The Gasoline Wars by Jean Thompson

Desirable Aliens by John Bovey
Naming Things by H. E. Francis
Transports and Disgraces by Robert Henson
The Calling by Mary Gray Hughes

Into the Wind by Robert Henderson
Breaking and Entering by Peter Makuck
The Four Corners of the House by Abraham Rothberg
Ladies Who Knit for a Living by Anthony E. Stockanes